THE AUTOBIOGRAPHY OF
MARY MAGDALENE

The Autobiography of Mary Magdalene

Beth Ingber-Irvin

ILLUSTRATIONS BY
Helen Hillix-Garcia

Blue Dolphin Publishing
1989

ISBN 0-931892-65-1

Library of Congress Catalog Card Number 89-80564

For information, address
Blue Dolphin Publishing, Inc.
P.O. Box 1908, Nevada City, CA 95959

Cover design: Dean Doss

Printed in the United States of America

9   8   7   6   5   4   3   2   1

Dedication

This book is dedicated to the earth and her healing.

Acknowledgments

I wish to thank Mary Magdalene, whose courage and love have illumined my way. I wish to thank my husband, who shares my way; my friends and partners, who clarify my way; and God, who is my way. I wish to thank my mother, who started me on my way. And, finally, I wish to thank Jesus, who, like the rest of us, is finding his way.

Foreword

This is the autobiography of Mary Magdalene, as recounted by her on her deathbed. Told in one night by a woman near death, the story may have some factual inaccuracies caused by the circumstances of the telling.

Mary foresaw the possibility of inaccuracies and was not concerned. Her passion was not facts, but truth, and as she said to me that night, "Too many facts blur the truth."

Being with Mary the night of her death changed my life. I believe it will change yours.

Beth Ingber-Irvin

שְׁמַע יִשְׂרָאֵל יְהֹוָה אֱלֹהֵינוּ יְהֹוָה אֶחָד:

"Hear, O Israel: The Lord our God, the Lord is one."
Deuteronomy 6:4

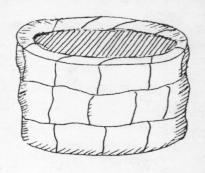

Chapter i

I'm afraid I'm making a mistake telling you of my life, committing myself to a story, a formulation that will pretend to encompass that which cannot be contained in words. Till this day, no one has been able to get that from me, a story that others will inevitably set in stone, a story that will be told and retold, a story that pretends to be true.

But I need, I ache to make peace with God before I die, so I am committing myself here to telling you the truth as I understand it, the truth of my life and my world. And by the truth I don't mean the facts, because too many facts blur the truth. No, I mean the truth, from the inside, what I know, what I saw, what I felt. And I am committing to explode my anger, my anger with Jesus, with God, with myself and with mankind, so that I can make peace with Jesus, with God, with myself, with mankind, so that I can release myself and God and the earth from the pain of my anger and the anger of my pain.

So I am willing to speak now, and I'm willing for you and everyone to hear, but I warn you that I don't wish to be interrupted or questioned until either I finish or die, whichever comes first.

And now let us begin.

Give me some water, won't you? Thank you.

1

My parched throat brings back memories of my childhood. It was very hot in the town of my birth, a town called
Nableze. Seven of us there were, seven children, and all
died in their first years except three: Naob, Martha and me.

Don't interrupt. I can see from your eyes you want to
question me. Leave the questions till after my death.

My father was not a wealthy man, not at that time. He
became quite well-to-do later, but only because of me. He
used my connections and capital to become a merchant, but
back then, we were farmers, and of farming, what I remember best is the goats.

My father was not a religious man, but he prayed on
Saturdays like all the other men, while my mother and I
made honeycakes at our home. I don't remember our home
very well. What a strange thing to forget. I don't remember
now if it was of stone. I think it was. All I remember clearly
is the well, and that wasn't at our house; it was a community
well, where I used to go every morning to gather water
while the roads were still cool on my feet.

But I'm straying. I want to tell you of my family. My
sister was two years older than I, but she had very little
ambition to go beyond my mother's role; always the good
little girl, she was. How could we confide in each other? I
despised her for accepting her lot, and she practically
shunned me so we would not be associated.

My brother was six years older than I, and it seemed he
was always out. My guess is that he was with my father,
travelling to lands that did not belong to us, but which our
family worked for a portion of the crop, which was sometimes good and sometimes bad. But for me, the crops didn't
matter. Some years there was more hunger, and some less.
But I don't recall receiving any finery in a good year, so I
don't suppose I missed any in a bad one.

2

My mother was more superstitious than religious, and she would often direct me to spit this way or that to ensure that the cakes would be good or the cloth well dyed. And the women would pray over food on Saturdays, and we would pray more intensely when there was a feast, which happened sometimes, and then we would eat goat with high seasonings.

Normally, however, it was the men who prayed, though we women never lost sight of the Almighty, because you didn't have to be a man to know that God was wondrous and awesome and quick to anger and slow to appease, that God demanded sacrifice and judged us harshly. And I laugh now, because there were so many learned folk not far from us in Bethlehem; yet we lived so isolated from modern thought, and our conception of God was not much deeper than our well.

I can't say my upbringing was either good or bad. My mother loved me, I know that. I was never sure of my father. What angered me most about him was that he was never there, or so it seemed. He and Naob, Naob and he, always coming and going, discussing, planning, leaving us women stuck at home, except that once a day I went to the well, and how far was that?

I thirsted for conversation and ideas. I, too, wished to talk to the Almighty and be heard by him. I despised to be unseen, to have to spit to gain his attention.

Sometimes I would ask my mother, "Do you think the Lord of the Universe is listening? is watching? Do you think we could converse?" And she would shrug her shoulders and continue to grind grain. "The Lord, God, King of the Universe, is busy listening to the men, and the Lord God is busy watching the children. And you, my dear, are almost twelve and not a child anymore, nor are you a man, so he's neither listening, nor watching but getting impatient because you are scalding the milk and ruining the dinner."

At twelve years old, I ran away. Do you blame me? All by myself, I went to Jerusalem, and that's the truth. I took some cakes, water and seeds, and I took some cloth, which I sold along the way. And I took on labor in people's homes and fields as well.

Six months it took me. Six months to walk to Jerusalem. I was terrified, perhaps even in shock. At night, sometimes I would sleep in the open fields, or by a stream, and I would tremble with fear that my father would find me, and I would tremble with fear that my father would not even be looking for me. And when I had been out two or three days and had not been found, I cried enough to fill all the village buckets, because I began to know and to be sure that He Who Rules the Universe not only does not listen or watch, he also does not care.

Because after three days, the night I heard the feet of men was not the night my father and brother came for me. It was the night the father and brother of another came for me and took me and gave me nothing in return. And I damned God for that, and I damn him still. And I wailed in fear and I wailed in pain, but not only did the Almighty not hear or watch; he did not care.

And the next morning, I found blood on my clothes, and with a bitterness no honeycake could ever disguise I placed my hands on my vagina, and I wept, and I vowed never to be taken or abused again. And with an agony that screams out to the universe yet today, I acknowledge that I have not been able to keep that vow, and I ache still to press a blade through my hand to release the pain that still rips within me, forever trapped in my thighs and my lips and my heart.

Because God abandoned me and I myself. And where was my father?

There have been many to accuse and to blame me. You, perhaps. Why was a young woman on the road, by herself, unprotected, seeking her fortune? How can I answer that? Because I could no longer tolerate making honeycake for those to whom God listened while God to me was deaf?

Or would you understand or even believe me, if I revealed that my brother had already approached me in the night and that I did not feel safe in that house?

What if I said that my father had many times touched me and forced me to touch him and that my mother was too tired from childbirths and miscarriages and deaths to care?

What if I told you I would rather be raped by a stranger than by my own family?

Would you be satisfied? Would you believe me? So leave it as I told you at first, not that I was found and raped by my father and brother, but that I was raped by two strangers and left for dead, that I was punished by God for abandoning my family and my kin, that I was Mary Magdalene and thus destined to be a whore.

Believe that, if you prefer.

Chapter ii

The Roman occupation never meant much to me before I went to live in Jerusalem. Twice a year the soldiers of Rome burst through my village and collected taxes, but the people's taxes had already been collected by the elders, so we had no direct contact with the army.

Besides, the Roman army wasn't really Roman, the soldiers seeming to be from everywhere else. So the fact that we were ruled by Rome had very little meaning to me.

While not impressed by the power of Rome, I was impressed by the power of their soldiers. They fascinated me. Men with different colors of hair and skin, men with strange uniforms and shields, men with swords, men whose sweat smelled different from the sweat of farmers.

I know I'm romanticizing. At that age, I was thrilled by raw power. And since the soldiers did not seem like a threat to me, I could enjoy the diversion they created in my life.

The occupation—was it real? Was it ever! But this I did not know till I came to Jerusalem that fine day, after six months of wandering, after six months of agony, crying, cursing, begging, working, thinking.

I was twelve and a half years old and pregnant. Was this child my father's, or was it my brother's? Or did it, perchance, belong to God Almighty himself? the bastard.

I remember the smell that greeted me as I carried myself heavily into the city. It was the smell of death. Roman executions. In those days, executions were a commonplace: men stabbed or crucified and abandoned on the roadside. Were they criminals? deserters? political opponents? thieves? rapists? accidental victims of drunken brawls? Were they, in fact, all killed by the Romans?

At first, I asked questions, but my neighbors in the tenements would look knowing but never say. I wonder sometimes if these folk said nothing because of their fear of the government, or because they themselves preferred to leave these murders uninvestigated. For their part, the Romans didn't care if all the deaths were attributed to them. Whether they committed these particular executions or not, the Romans loved to be feared.

The day I entered Jerusalem, the first smell that greeted me may have been death, but the second was life. In the tenements, life smelled like childbirth and garbage and sweet wine and incense and roasted sesame seeds and sex and anger and piety and urine and sheep.

I was from the country and not squeamish. I was used to all kinds of smells, but I was sickened by their concentration. Too many people, too many goats, too much pain, too much life, too much death.

My first day in Jerusalem, I found a friend, a man with dirty toenails and foul breath, a man who fancied me as a daughter. At least, partly.

Jacob was his name, and he lived in a tenement building in the heart of the city. Most tenements at that time contained several apartments, each apartment consisting of four or five rooms, one room opening to the other, like beads strung together. The rooms were quite small, and each was filled with five to ten related or unrelated people, depending on the size of the family and the size of their means.

Jacob let me stay with him and seven other men, women and children in one of these rooms. God, the stench! Yet there was another smell that first night, the smell of roasting lamb. And I got to eat some of it. We all ate, every one of us. Lamb. Whose lamb was it? Someone, some one among us had gotten hold of a lamb, and we all shared. It was marvelous. As I ate, I felt myself lifted physically and in spirit, touched by the sacrifice of that lamb, the lamb's sacrifice of its life for me, for us, for my baby. I was touched. I was struck. I was in awe of the wonder of one life given for another.

Perhaps it was at this moment that I began to connect to God, to let go of some of my anger and pain. In this overly warm room, full of foul-smelling people, I was filled with sustenance, and I was sustained.

We drank a little wine. It was the sabbath. I felt my fear of my new life, yet I also felt my hope. Blessed be the Lord, King of the Universe, who sustains us through the fruit of the earth, the fruit of the vine. Amen.

Do you think my spiritual awakening a bit abrupt? Understand that these thoughts are in retrospect. My first day with Jacob was full of fear and defiance toward God. Only years later did I understand that my softening towards God began with that meal, with someone's act of generosity.

Jacob was religious and kind, the kindest man I had ever met. I wish I could remember him better, that I could recount to you tales of his life, how he came to have such dirty feet, but it eludes me now.

8

"You are a good child," he would say to me, as we settled down to sleep on that grimy floor. "Blessed are the children that knoweth not temptation. More blessed are the children that knoweth."

Jacob, I miss you! Gone, dead, I imagine. So many years! How can we lose track of those souls that touch our path and help us stay alive until God heals us? For that is what Jacob did for me. I believed nothing of his religion; his love of God was like a spur under my feet. Yet that first night, when he took me in and I ate lamb, I sensed that someday I would feel loved by God. And until then I would be no less and no more, only more empty.

And so it was. Amen.

Jacob. He loved hazelnuts and ate them whenever he could. And when he could not, he ate seeds. The mat on which we lay together was always full of shells. That I remember, the feeling of hard shells under my swollen body. And Jacob.

I suppose I'm avoiding telling you something, something very painful.

She died, my baby. I gave birth in less than nine months. One of the women in the next room came to help and comfort me, but it was no use. She died.

The next day, Jacob disappeared. Why? Had he cared for me only for the baby? Had he cherished me only because of her?

Jacob, why did you go? and where? Did you ever exist, or were you a dream that I created to lessen the pain of those terrible days?

God! God! I cannot forget the death of my child, my firstborn, my baby girl. I cry to you today. I ask your pity for her and for me. Why could we not have been together throughout this miserable life?

At moments I have peace about her death. What would I have done with such a momentous responsibility? I who was not yet thirteen? who had no money, no prospects, no relations, no love for myself, no experience, no home. What could I have done with this bastard child of an incestuous union?

At moments, I have peace about it and believe that my life required a freedom to come and go, to choose the harder road, to love only God. Yet at other moments, I remember the anguish, and I am not at peace.

I never saw Jacob again. And now without my baby, and now without him, and now without pity for myself or anyone, I began again and ate the dirt and survived.

Chapter iii

This is a hard thing, telling you the story of my life. I want to tell my side, to justify myself. Yet I want to be fair, as well.

For instance, have I been fair to Jacob? What have I really told you about him? Did I tell you that just before I gave birth, he brought me a pomegranate and that a pomegranate was a treasure, because I had so little fruit, and I always felt thirsty?

Is it important that Jacob brought me a pomegranate? More important than that he left me just after the child was born dead?

Give me some water now. I can still feel that thirst, that desert thirst. How can you ever understand it?—the thirst that comes upon you when you are away from a secure source of water, the thirst for something cool and wet, for fruit?

My mind is wandering. I'm sorry. I want to be fair to God, I don't know why. Perhaps it's just vanity. I want you to know that in those dark days, I was healing, that it was all part of God's plan, that the plan in itself proves that God acknowledged me, always acknowledged me.

My motive for telling you may be vanity, but the truth is that I was healing. When Jacob acknowledged my existence, cared for me, I began to trust that so could God. When I existed to Jacob, I existed to myself, even to God—I, who was neither a man nor a child.

After Jacob, I moved out of the tenement into a big house where I was a servant. At that house I saw four daughters being doted on by their father, and yes, I felt envy and anger and hate. But I also felt glad, because I saw four daughters who existed in the eyes of their father and, therefore, in the eyes of God. And I began to believe that love for me could exist, too—the love of a man, the love of God.

Can you understand? I feel so frustrated, tired, sick and muddled, and I'm afraid you won't see how I could be in the depths of despair and in the pit of agony and know in that moment the potential for light, how I could feel God's love in the sacrifice of the lamb for me, in Jacob's care for me, in the care that other daughters received from their fathers.

I want you to see that though I was emptied when I lost my baby, and I was envious and hateful, even my bitterness healed me as it led me to rage and through rage to a sense of deserving that I had never had before. And when, later, Jesus touched my hand and offered me the kingdom of heaven, I knew I had the right, no matter what I had done. And I would never have known that had I stayed in my mother's house and been counted as less than nothing.

Vanity or not, I want you to understand this. And now I will go on.

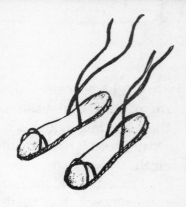

Chapter iv

I'm going to tell you now about my years as the servant of Menachem ben Israel, his wife and four daughters.

After the baby's death, I needed a safe place to go, and I needed to get away from the tenement, from the dirt, the danger and the death.

I was not yet thirteen, with no connections, but I found a position as a servant in a rich house. You may think that a servant is rather a lowly job, but to me it was a haven. I shared a room with only one other girl, and we all lived in an enormous mansion that was in the Roman style. There was a lot of water, a lot of water, and sometimes I ate fruit, which the family kept in abundance. Everywhere there was the smell of rose water, and I was dressed very clean.

At first, I had only my coarse country smock, and I was given nothing else to wear because I washed floors in the servants' quarters. But later I advanced into the main part of the house, and I was given lovely things to wear, and that was important, because it helped me to begin to feel beautiful.

Menachem ben Israel was the father of four daughters, four spoiled daughters. His wife, Naomi, was very vain and at the same time ineffectual. She spent a lot of time on herself and her friends and very little time on her daughters.

13

But he, my God, there was nothing he would not give them. I remember sneaking into their rooms and eyeing their sandals, which smelled of exotic woods. Sometimes I would touch their clothes, which were made of the finest cloth.

I hated them, the daughters. The youngest, Rachel, was rather sweet, but petulant. She had curly hair and eyelashes, and though only six years old when I arrived at the house, already she could order anyone around.

Ruth was the oldest, and she was more like the woman of the house than a daughter. She controlled her father, dominated her mother and commanded her sisters.

She was bitter, and I liked that, because it made me feel justified in being bitter, too. In the end, she was also the saddest, because she never married and felt abandoned when her charges did.

In between were Nachuma and another girl, whose name escapes me. Their personalities are not quite so vivid in my memory, although I knew them all again in later life.

I feel a certain smugness, as I share all this with you. I want you to know that later in life I surpassed those four daughters, I who had started as a lowly servant, I who was despised by them. I want you to know that ten years later I was their father's lover and later yet, I was a leader of Jewish women and a power to be reckoned with.

It embarrasses me to admit that I am so vain, that any of this is or ever was important to me. And it embarrasses me to admit that it angered me that they never acknowledged me, I who became such a leader.

I think they never forgave me for becoming their father's lover, that they never forgave me for being my own woman. I suppose I never forgave them for having been so pampered, for having had power over me, for having been loved.

There have been times when I have felt so cloaked by the love of God that I have been without a trace of bitterness or vanity. But such a state of mind is not always with me. Forgive me.

In truth, those children were not loved. Abandoned by their mother, abused by their sister and dominated by their father, pampered but powerless, they never found themselves, even as adults. Lacking a sense of themselves, they lacked the power to break from their family, break from their class, join us and follow their hearts to God. That is sad. I hope they have found love, self-respect and peace.

But that is me now. When I tended them at their father's house, I only hurt.

What I have to say now makes me feel ill. I don't want to tell you. I fear, I don't know what. My own judgment? The judgment of God? Surely God knows everything about me—what I admit, what I do not.

And you, I can see from your eyes that you will love me no matter what I say about myself. But this. . . .

Do I hesitate to speak because I fear other women, their condemnation? Do I believe that I, Mary Magdalene, must prove who I am by hiding who I have been?

I wish to walk beyond my fears today. I am to die soon, very soon. I am myself, in my full worth. I have been a human woman, walking on this earth, full of pain. I have been and still am divine, a piece of God with thighs and breasts and a heart that has beheld God and been awed, that has beheld God's pain and been moved.

I want you to forgive me. I molested a child, the child whose name I pretend to forget. I molested Basya. She was but nine years old and I fifteen, now a trusted servant in the house of the whoremonger.

Her father had been molesting me. He took liberties with many of the servants, touching the girls' breasts and thighs, forcing the men to touch him, and he took liberties with me.

Sometimes I feel ashamed to reveal, to admit, how many men had sex with me when I was young, how many men molested me. I'm afraid you will think somehow it was my fault. I don't know. Perhaps it was. Perhaps it was my youth, my vulnerability, my need for love and protection.

I suppose you want to know if Jacob was among them. Well, perhaps he was. Will you think, ah, there again, Mary Magdalene, unable to have a relationship with a man without having sex? Will you smirk and say, we know why she became a prostitute?

I deny nothing! I am tired of denial. I was a victim. I wasn't a victim. I found myself abused at every turn; I found myself an abuser as well. I became a prostitute to make the abusers pay. Maybe it gave me a sense of power to have men want me, pay for me.

But you will know, you must know, as I tell you my story how hard a road I walked, how much I paid for the little power I thought I had.

But, here, I am straying from this most painful part, the most painful part of my life. I stole into her room. I went to Basya at night when she slept, and I placed one hand over her face so she could neither cry nor weep nor see, and with the other hand, I roughly touched her the way her father touched me. And I was bitter. So very, very bitter.

In a moment, I came to myself, and I fled so quickly that the startled child could not realize exactly what had happened. And she began to cry.

Where was her nurse? you are probably asking. Where was this spoiled rich child's nurse? Her nurse! Her nurse was right there. It was I! I was her nurse.

And I rushed in to calm her and to quiet her. And I said she must have had a bad dream. But she insisted not, insisted that something had happened. And in the morning I admitted that I had strayed for just a moment to take care of some personal need and that in that moment she must have been attacked.

And the frantic father questioned everyone. Had they seen anyone in the halls, in the stairwells, in the gardens? But no one had seen anything. Finally a new male servant was accused and whipped and discharged with no proof and no mercy. And I, I felt sickened by what I had done and begged for forgiveness for not having protected the child. Yet I was barely reprimanded. For I was trusted. Or perhaps, it was that the father feared to know.

And no one, no one, not even the child herself, ever suggested that I, a girl, could have done what only men were meant to do.

And shortly thereafter I resigned. I left to find my calling on the street. I, who have never before told anyone but Jesus about what I had done, went out to punish myself and my sexuality for what I had done in anger to another child.

And only so many years later, when Jesus and I sat with love as our bond, when I felt his compassion and understanding, did I begin to forgive myself and was I freed forever of my need to use or be used, was I freed forever of my need to punish myself or the men who drove me to such a place of self-contempt.

And now I am telling you and through you, the world. And this dark moment of my life is and always will be a deep part of my need for God's love and forgiveness, and thus is and always will be my direct channel to God and to the divine.

And I am glad I have told you, because it was you whom I molested.

Amen.

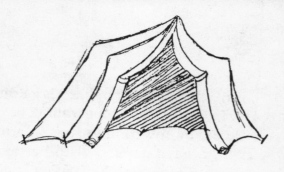

Chapter v

Oh....I must have dozed off. What time is it? I'm sorry. I hope you haven't been sitting there long, waiting for me.

Just a little water, perhaps, and help me sit up more. And, please, don't let me fall asleep on you again.

So, where was I? Yes, I remember. I was fifteen, wasn't I? fifteen when I left the house of Menachem ben Israel, his wife and four daughters.

I suppose you want to know about my years as a prostitute. Everyone does. I'll tell you. Why not? It's part of my life. But I will tell you only what I want to recount, not what you want to hear. Agreed?

The story begins with Sarah, my first real friend. I met her in the market one day, when I was helping Ruth shop. We loved each other immediately, and I often snuck off to see her, when I could get away. Naturally, when I left the ben Israel house, I hoped for Sarah's help.

Sarah was beautiful, so beautiful, I can feel the richness of her body in my blood, even now. A shopkeeper's daughter, not a prostitute, she worked in the market with her father, Nathan. She was wild. Her mother had died when she was first born, and from then on she was raised only by her father. They lived and worked together selling this and that, sometimes more this than that; sometimes more that than this.

I'm rambling. My rambling is getting worse. I had better hurry before I can no longer think or recount the tale.

To Sarah, my coming was an adventure, so she was excited to have me stay with her and her father on the outskirts of town. But he, Nathan, was a jealous man. He was jealous of our girlish giggles and our love for each other, jealous of our secrets and caresses, jealous of his daughter. So he forced me to leave. And Sarah, my beloved friend, she did not fight him. I have always blamed him, but the truth is that she abandoned me, too. I suppose the truth is that more than he, she was to blame, because she let him, let him force me to leave.

Sarah, I wish you had come with me! had had the courage to leave, to run, to trust yourself, to be hurt. Well, she didn't. But as it happened, during those few days before I was made to leave, Sarah had introduced me to Miriam, Miriam Aboudou, and that was how my new life began.

Miriam had a tent, also on the outskirts of the city, and she had shared it with another girl. The girl had recently died of cholera, so she was glad to have another mate. I suppose it seems absurd of me to put it so, but in some ways, you know, she was my mate, another being with whom I could share my life, whatever that life was. And Miriam and I shared everything.

What did I think of my life? At that time? Truthfully, at first, I was quite excited. I was finally free. No mother to try to bend my thoughts to hers. And no man—neither father, nor employer, nor even dear Jacob—no man to own me. Furthermore, I had money, and money gave me independence.

To me, money was payment for degradation. From childhood, I had felt degraded. As a whore, I finally had the self-respect to demand payment for it.

20

Miriam showed me all the ropes: how to keep myself clean (that was a fetish with me); how to prevent babies; how to abort, if the copper failed to keep me without child; how to bargain; how to make an unwilling man pay; how to pay a man back if he hurt me.

Sometimes, in the morning, when we rested and slept, Miriam and I would lie in bed together, and she would tell me stories of her life, not only in the tent, but also back home. Miriam was very dark, much more so than I, and she came from far away. When just a child, she had been separated from her family through war. After that, she had been traded several times, always moving north, until some merchants brought her to Jerusalem by ship and by road. She was going into service with a wealthy family, when she escaped. By luck, she met an older girl who took her in for a percentage of her income, and she set up her business when she was eleven years old.

Frankly, I don't know how much of her story to believe. But she was surely a very experienced girl when I met her.

I loved her, and she, me. We often held each other and kissed and soothed each other's heart and body. And we had no secrets, except her scars. She had deep scars on her body and on her face. She never spoke about them, and I never asked. Yet I suppose they frightened me and made me respect her more.

You may be surprised that we could work together in the same tent, but it was really quite easy. We each had a cot behind a screen, and it was comforting to know that the other was there. Once or twice, it probably saved my life.

How I felt about the men, that's hard to explain. Sometimes they frightened me; usually they repelled me; always they excited me—at first. The excitement was like the childhood thrill I had had when the Roman army had come through our town. Their hardness, their smell, gave me the feeling, no, more the illusion, that the men were strong, that they could save me from my father, that they could protect me from God, himself.

I suppose that excitement and hope played a big part at first. Soon, though, the excitement faded, and all that remained was the disgust, and the coins.

I remember some of those men so clearly. I had many regular customers—merchants, soldiers, artisans, priests. But the one I remember most clearly was a man who came just once and left a deep mark on me.

He was a soldier, a Roman soldier from Rome, not from here or there, who came to my tent, seeking me out personally. He wore a helmet that covered the whole front of his face. And he was rich; he wore gold all over his body.

But it was not because of his wealth that I remember him. I remember him because of the helmet that he wore over his face, because of the helmet that he kept over his face, over his mouth, even as he came to me. And I remember him because he kissed me, and he forced me to kiss him through the helmet covering his face, and he forced me to kiss his mouth through the helmet, through my pain and through my tears. And I cried out, but Miriam was not there, and I said no, but he forced me, forced me to kiss him through the helmet, the cold metal bruising my lips, and he bit my mouth and sucked it into his, through the metal, through that harsh opening, through the helmet that covered his face. And I felt sick, ice cold sick, and he pressed my mouth through that opening, holding my face prisoner with his hands, my mouth against sharp metal, and I tried to push him away, but I could not pull my mouth from that helmet that covered his face.

Then suddenly he threw me back on my cot and ripped off the helmet, and I saw his lips bleeding and his eyes commanding, and he demanded that I suck his penis with my bleeding mouth, and I thought about the well in my home town, how deep it was, how cool and refreshing the water, how I would bathe my lips in the cool water of that refreshing well and walk home in the early morning and hear the goats and plot my escape, and eat seeds and cut my lips on the shells and dream of God and my lover and smear honey on my mouth and wash away my tears and be loved.

What was it like? What do you think it was like? Men coming and going, infections, fear, humiliation, anger, revenge. I wanted so much to make men pay, and I did; but I paid more. I paid more.

And Miriam and I laughing when we could. Cherishing sleep.

Chapter vi

I suppose I want to skip over some parts, but your eyes won't let me, will they?

I have to talk about the baby, don't I? My baby.

Are you surprised, with all my precautions, that I got with child again? Don't be. It was common enough. I had used my specially blessed copper coin, but it had betrayed me, or I it. I don't know. Had I been sloppy in its insertion? Did I meet a man whose will was too strong to be thwarted by my efforts?

Whatever the reason, I became pregnant and I refused an abortion. I wanted the baby.

I was seventeen years old and as big as our tent. And I continued to work, because, you know, there's always men, no matter how you look or how pregnant you are.

And somehow I talked Miriam into letting me stay, and even into keeping the baby, too. And we made plans for raising her (it had to be another baby girl, I just knew it).

And I was sick, so sick. At times I felt I would die, with men's foul limbs pinning me down and with vomit wanting to burst through my lips and into their ugly faces. The men. I hated them then. I had lost all my tolerance for them. I had lost, too, all hope of their strong arms, all hope that some-one, just one, would save me, rescue me, adore me, change my life, elevate me, be tender with me.

The meek ones. You probably think they were better. They weren't, just more deceitful.

I wanted that baby. And so did Miriam. I believe to this day that we would have loved that baby and honored it.

It died. I don't know why. Some fat man, probably. I was seven months pregnant. It died.

I don't want to talk about it anymore.

You are probably wondering about God, why I don't mention God. You are right to ask.

The truth is that in those years, I thought very little about God. I had no belief anymore that I could or would be rescued by men. And I suspect that at the same moment I lost faith in God. The God who had given me lamb the first night I came to Jerusalem, he was gone, drowned in semen.

Oh there were some prostitutes who remembered God each time they spread their legs. They thanked God for their business, thanked God for not being dead, thanked God for a successful abortion, thanked God for their daily misery.

Not I. Not I.

God, you must remember those terrible days that we spent together, so intimately connected, yet so far apart in my mind. You must remember, God, because I remember, remember how little I remembered you and acknowledged your place in my life. Of course I had Miriam. Perhaps she had taken your place. Perhaps you had given her to me so that she would. Miriam. I loved her. She loved me. Yet she stole from me, God. She stole my money when she thought I was asleep. And I let her.

You laugh, God. I suppose at that time I believed that you had to pay for everything. Indeed, I did. . .pay for everything.

My baby was dead, but I was not. At eighteen years old, I looked at my tent, I smelled myself, and I was appalled. I wanted something more.

I had to leave Miriam. I had to focus on my ambition, not on our relationship. I had to save money, not let it be stolen.

I had to learn how to use men and be powerful in a way that Miriam never fathomed.

I had to get out of the tent, out of the stinking outskirts of town. I had to find my way to the heart, to the center of life. I had to—no, I wanted to have power, money, influence, respect. I wanted to know the world. I wanted to prove my mother wrong.

No, I hadn't done that yet. As far as I could see, God still neither heard nor saw me. I wanted to be seen, to be heard, even to be feared by men, by God. . . .

One afternoon I awoke and packed my things. I did not kiss Miriam, because I would have felt her love, her need and my own, and I would have stayed. I had not one idea as to what I would do, but I was determined to make a place for my crying spirit in the universe that ignored or shat on me. I would.

Chapter vii

You know, Beth, I'm getting quite used to talking to you. I suppose that will help both of us. Your question about Miriam, was she from Ghana? I don't know. She came from a place south and west, on the other side of the Sahara. I wasn't well versed in geography then, and, indeed, we had different ways of viewing the world, too.

You see, we talked about peoples more than places. Jerusalem at the time was like a carpet woven of different tribes, sects, races. Miriam and I, for example, we lived east of the city proper in a tent community inhabited by Berbers. I liked that; so did she. We had no one from our own societies to watch us, to impose upon us values or social rules that felt uncomfortable. We were able, almost, to create our own world.

Almost, I say, because we carry our old world inside us, don't we? For while the God of Abraham seemed in our tent less omnipresent than he had seemed in the Jewish tenements, he still haunted my nightmares and he still shaped my dreams. Yes, after all those years, I still dreamed to be seen and heard by Jehovah, the God of the Jews, and nothing else would satisfy that need.

Why didn't Miriam come with me? It is time for me to confess to you that I have lied about some things, some things about Miriam. Oh, I did not want to lie to you, but I promised Miriam many years ago that all her secrets would be safe with me.

It's time now for truth, for all truth. I did know about Miriam, about her home and about her scars.

Miriam was from southern Egypt, but she had taken an exotic name to hide that fact. Her father was a sheikh, a power among his own people, and he had many wives. When Miriam was very young, her mother was killed by another of her father's wives, a young woman filled with jealousy and fear, a woman vainly seeking power through the killing of a rival.

Miriam wanted to avenge her mother's death. She blamed not the other woman, who acted out of her own pitiful lack of power. She blamed her father, who sought more wives than he could honor and bless.

Miriam, quite frankly, tried to seduce her father. She saw lust as his weakness, and she hoped to seduce and shame him in that way; she hoped to shame him, and she hoped to denounce him. It was a foolish and childish plot, dreamed up in the mind of a grieving, powerless young girl. And it was an arrogant plot as well, one which stamped the pattern of her life.

She was but ten years old, but she darkened her eyes, wore her mother's gold and clothes and went to her father's bed, whispering her passion in his ear. She hoped her beauty and sensuality would arouse him, hoped he would not care who she was, hoped he would be ensnared, hoped she would become pregnant with his child.

Her father recognized her at once, not because he knew her face, but because he knew her mother's things. To her amazement, he threw her from his bed. It was against his beliefs to whore his own daughter.

Miriam, Miriam. She felt tremendous shame, not for what she had done, but for her failure to avenge her mother's death. And for this failure, she blamed herself. Miriam, Miriam. And in her anguish, she scarred her own face and body, punishing them for their inability to entrap her father. When I think of it, a ten-year-old child knifing her own face and limbs. . . .

When her father saw her mutilated face and body, he sold her. He never asked why. He was a coward. Or, perhaps, he felt the shame, after all. And that is the story.

Miriam would never leave that tent. In the tent she could hide; in the tent she could daily and nightly seduce the man who rejected her and caused her shame. In the tent, she could live with her bitterness.

Miriam would never leave that tent, and Miriam tried to stop me from leaving, too. She stole my money to keep me there; she tried to seduce me to keep me there; she encouraged my fear to keep me there. But she could not. I am sure this caused her more shame.

Miriam killed herself a few years after I left. But I went on.

I knew I had to leave, but I didn't know where to go. Even among the Jews, we were many tribes, many subgroups, many sects. I could have joined a small group of struggling souls from my old village, but I shunned them, feeling that they, too, were ignored by God. I could have returned to the service of the Pharisees, who were powerful, indeed, but among them I had no chance of status.

After much thought, I decided to join a group whose name has been long forgotten, but which was famous for the power of its woman priests. This may amaze you, but the heart of the sect was a brothel in the southeast part of the city.

A fine, strong woman named Judith Aziba ran the house and was the priestess. She had incredible magic, both sexual and nonsexual, and she was powerful among both the Jews and the Romans. She was in the center, acknowledged by God, and this was where I wished to be.

When I returned to Jerusalem, I had no choice but to go back to the tenements and work there for several months. But I desperately wanted to be accepted by Aziba, and I made plans to petition to be initiated as her student and as a member of her household.

Aziba was famous among the tenement- and tent-dwelling prostitutes, because she had power and respect, money and magic. All her women were beautiful, educated and skilled in sexual, political and social matters. Used, bitter, ignorant and crude, I had very little reason to expect her acceptance. Yet never did I give up the idea that I would succeed in joining her.

Sometimes foolishness and ambition inspire us to the good. After several months of working and saving, I went to the house where she lived and taught, and I sat in the anteroom, begging the servants to arrange for an interview. I was by that time almost nineteen, and despite my rough life, I had a compelling physical beauty which I hoped would open doors for me.

She never came; she never looked. I had no chance to tell her that I, too, shared her vision of powerful women; that I hated men and wanted them put in their place; that I was ready to worship her if only she would take me as her student.

She never came; she never heard; she had no chance to be swayed by my beauty, adoration or sincerity or by the offer of all my savings as a dowry to gain me entrance to her domain.

She did not come, and she did not meet me. But as though she knew who I was, through a servant she sent me a reply. Beth, you cannot imagine my shock and amazement, confusion, bitterness, hope and anguish, when I received her message.

I was to go to the desert and rid myself of my rage. And when I was barefoot, without clothing, money or vanity, I was to return to her door and offer myself as her student.

I hope you are laughing with me. I was, of course, enranged by this idea. I wanted to be elevated, not denigrated; encouraged, not mortified; admired, not belittled. I wanted access to power; and I wanted it now.

I returned to the tenements and worked furiously for nine more months. In those months, I concentrated on money, bought beautiful clothes, a mantle of deep rose and a dress with gold threads. I bought a room for myself from an old man whose wife had died and who was returning to the country. I bought frankincense and myrrh. I bought lamb and goat.

And I felt humiliated, because I was prostituting myself to God. I tried to make him see me and hear me through my clothes, my beauty, my success and my cleverness. He never did.

One morning, I awoke from another night of empty dreams. I was nineteen, going on twenty. I felt alone; I had no one's love. I had been in Jerusalem since I was twelve years old, and I was no closer to the center of the universe than I had been when I dragged my pregnant body past the row of crucifixes and smelled the life and death here in the city.

So I did it. I gave away everything that I had earned, had broken my back for. I gave it away and went to the desert.

Believe me or not. It is so.

Amen.

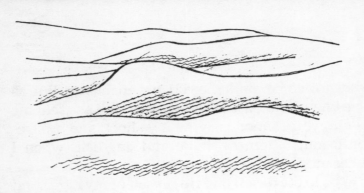

Chapter viii

I didn't have a clue, not a clue as to what to do. I hated God, yet had to ask for God's direction. I hated Aziba, yet had no other guide. With just enough money to keep me alive, I travelled south seeking a way, a place to let go of my rage.

Oh, Lord, what a sense of humor you have. Not a day out of town and I was robbed! I wanted so badly to curse God and Aziba. What had they done to me? Why the hell was I doing this, anyway? Why would any woman want to let go of her rage? Why would I? Why would she ask me to? I wanted to be a courtesan in her brothel; I wanted respect and a place in God's eyes. For this, why did I need to be without rage?

And if I were to be helped with my rage, why did the Almighty, Blessed Is He, have me robbed, leave me confused and rageful on the side of the road, with nowhere to go and no one to ask?

Why the hell didn't God talk to me? Apologize for the theft? Ask my forgiveness for the pain I had suffered, for the loss of my babies, for the rapes, for the brutalization? It was God, not I, that needed humility, correction, revelation. It was God that needed to let go of his anger and abuse toward women.

And why would a woman, Aziba, ask me to do this? She was supposed to be my champion, not a collaborator with an ancient vengeful God, who had hurt me.

You know, Beth, with all the pain that I had known in my life, I had rarely cried. I had cried when I lost my babies. I had cried when my father and brother raped me on the road to Jerusalem. I had cried when I found myself alone, back in the tenements after I left Miriam.

But to cry, openly, for hours, to let God see how pained I had become, to let anyone see how weak I was, to allow myself to know how small I felt, no, I could not, would not let be pierced the membrane of pride that, more than my hymen, fiercely hid my self, my womb-deep flesh and soul, my spirit and my heart, my pain.

But that day, with all the spirits tearing at me—wanting to run back to the tenement, to Miriam, to my mother; wanting to kill Aziba, God, Jacob, you, myself; wanting to wrench from my heart the need to be seen by God, to be important, to be loved—that day, with all the spirits tearing at me, I crumbled, and I began to weep.

And I staggered wailing into the desert, with only my tears to quench my thirst, and I wailed to my mother to love me, and I wailed to my father to love me, and I wailed to the Almighty, damn his name, to love me. And I wept, and I wept, and I ate sand as it battered my mouth and eyes. And I ripped at my flesh to blot from my knowing the pain in my groin and in my heart. And I cried. I cried. I cried.

Fourteen days I cried. Fourteen days I cursed. Fourteen days I begged to God to take me in his arms and give me peace. Fourteen days I was delirious, clinging to rocks to stay on the earth through the wind and the storms.

Fourteen days I vomited pain and bitterness, anger, hope and despair. All the feelings and wants of a young girl,

33

a young woman, vomited and vomited until I was so empty I cared not whether I was seen or heard. I cared only not to care.

And after fourteen days, one morning, I sat, dazed, as the sun rose. And I laughed, because in that moment, I did not care. And a great peace came over me.

I cannot, or do not always carry that peace, but I know it exists. It is a state of being that I can visit often. And as I have been telling you my story, I am brought back to those days in the desert, because I feel this telling to be a similar moment for me, a time of vomiting whatever is left in my heart's heart of the pain and the anger, the anger and the pain, so that I can be forever without rage, so that I can embrace my life fully, so that I can know love.

And already I can feel that soon I will be completely at peace, Beth, at peace, Beth, at peace.

Chapter ix

What keeps a woman like me going? What a funny question. What keeps you going?

I came back to Jerusalem, and like a dog that is every day brought to the same place and returns by rote even without its master, I returned to the house of Aziba. By then, I barely cared if she accepted me or not. Half dead, I sat in her anteroom, spoke with no one and waited with no anticipation.

It was not a moment before she, herself, emerged. I had never seen her before; and even as I sat there worn and nearly crazed, I was amazed and dazzled by what I saw. Her magnificent dark head, her crimson robe, her headdress of aromatic herbs, her serpentine jewelry, her sandaled feet—she was so sure of herself, so proud. I wanted to fall to her feet and smell her womanly parts.

What a magic moment for me. Without my having identified myself or petitioned for her acceptance, she had greeted me with abundant love and jubilation, as though she knew me and had been waiting for me.

"Mary, at last you have come to me," she said. How dizzy I felt. How did she know me? What did she see but a battered body?

With the tenderest touch but the deepest strength, Aziba leaned my body upon hers, unconcerned for her crimson robe or her white garments, her hair or her skin. And she took me gently and with deftness into a suite, which she said was mine and had always been mine. And she bathed me with rose water, and she washed my hair with herbs, and she treated my parched and burned skin with an ointment that smelled of cloves, and she brought me millet flavored with coconut and bade me eat, slowly and carefully.

Oh, Aziba, you saved my life that day. You gave me hope. You filled me with love of my womanness. You quenched my thirst for gentleness and renewal. I will never forget your care and your enlightenment, your love and your detachment, your willingness to let me face the harshest days and your ability to heal.

I thank God for you, Aziba, and I thank you for God, because with you began the move toward a God that encompasses all things and is all being; a God who does not hold me in his arms and give me peace, because he does not own the arms that hold me or own the peace that I crave; a God who cannot abandon because he does not embrace; a God that neither sees me nor is blind to me because he is me; a God with whom I am the center because there is only the center. Amen.

My days of power and joy began that morning, or so it seemed, for, of course, they had begun many days, many years, many centuries before. I discovered that my arduous preparation for Aziba's acceptance was unique among her students, that I had received "special treatment" because she had seen me in a dream and had known what I needed to become myself.

Aziba, personally, became my teacher, as well as my friend. She taught me her ceremonial magic, her sacred dance; she taught me to become the wind, the water, the earth, the sky; she taught me to speak to everyone with confidence and without shame; she taught me to renew my body; she taught me to renew my soul. Yet I was a prostitute.

You cannot understand this, I can see. In order to do so, you must understand our times. We had so very few choices then, so very few ways to walk without the support of men. We were not women supported by wealthy fathers; we did not wish to be wives supported by wealthy husbands. We chose a profession where our financial support was diverse and so not oppressive, where the men who paid us could not own us.

And from this place of self-empowerment came the basis of our self-realization.

As Aziba's special student and friend, I was given every opportunity to learn and develop myself, so it was not long before I was very much sought after, and soon I was able to change my life. I built a house next to Aziba's, where I trained young women who joined us. Having to entertain very few men myself, I could enjoy a life of teaching, study, meditation and dance.

One of the men I did permit into my company was Menachem ben Israel. Was my motive some strange form of revenge? He did not at first know me. But, later, his daughter Rachel recognized me and he came to realize who I was. He feared me. He feared my power as a woman, my knowledge of who he really was. Life's ironies.

But there is another part of this story that is extremely important, important because it explains so much of my history and the history of our sect. It is the story of intrigue, of politics, of being in the center or close to the center of men's world.

Aziba was renowned not only for her magic, but for her intelligence and connections. Our houses were an instrument for the transmission of secrets and missives among the various factions of Jerusalem politics. The Romans had to respect the power of the Jewish political and judicial infrastructure; and both had to respect the power of the many other nationalities housed in our city and throughout our land.

There were primitive Europeans, Sumarians, Indians, Persians, Greeks, Ethiopians, and so on. Some groups, such as the Jews and the Persians, were semi-autonomous; others were too weak in number, social development or economic power to be forces in themselves.

Of all the nationalities, the Jews, or the Israelites, were the most powerful and the most autonomous. The occupation government had to appear to govern us without instigating us to rebellion. To be either too harsh or too lax would not only unravel the delicate relationship between the Israelites and the Romans, it might unleash anarchy among the less politically developed minorities. Another of life's ironies: with all its armies and proclamations and symbols of power, Roman rule in Israel was weak, indecisive and, perhaps inevitably, uncertain of itself.

Aziba and I had our role. We arranged many secret meetings; we were also entrusted with communications that neither side dared openly acknowledge.

We could do this because we were seen as neutral and trustworthy by both sides. Our sect was not officially recognized by the Sanhedrin, so the Romans were able to maintain the fiction that we were not Jewish. While they may have doubted the truth of this fiction, it was convenient for them, and principles were not important to an empire trying to maintain its existence.

The Sanhedrin, too, counted on our ambiguous status. On their behalf, we could act outside the strict constraints of Jewish law. Yet we were not non-Jews and so could be trusted. Extremely tolerant of sectarian differences among themselves, the Jews of the time felt a deep kinship with one another. Behind smiles and behind winks, the powerful Jews could send us off to communicate with the Romans without fear of betrayal.

I laugh now about some of the secrets we kept. Things which appeared important then seem ludicrous now, over the distance of time and miles. Yet, I suppose, many lives, many ambitions were at stake, empire was at stake, and the game itself was at stake—the political game, the game where we challenge God to a test of wills.

My political role has long ceased to seem significant to me, yet I must acknowledge that at the time, it vastly contributed to my security and well-being. I knew a great deal about a great number of people, and as long as my discretion was unquestionable, I was seen and, therefore, was a very powerful woman. I also loved the role for the role itself. From an ignorant country girl, to a tent-dwelling whore, to a mid-city prostitute, to a priestess wielding power among men, my ascent dazzled me.

I loved it. But in the political game, there is always a risk, and you will see how, later, I almost lost my life.

May I have some broth? You know, I feel much stronger in this moment. I have so enjoyed telling you my story, I have lost the sense of impending delerium. I have become clearer, haven't I? I thought so. And just a drop of broth will help me go on with the tumultuous years ahead.

But first I have to tell you about the growing strain between Aziba and me. When I came to her, I worshipped and adored her, and she was in every way worthy of my love, gratitude and respect.

But Aziba had her path, and I had mine.

Aziba taught us survival—how to stay centered despite the mutual abuse and exploitation we engaged in with men. The technique was detachment, detachment from our need

39

for love in every relationship, detachment from our bodies' sensitivity to touch, detachment from the pain of wives or lovers who were being betrayed by our clients through us, detachment from the jealousy of our competition.

I learned to detach. I was proud. I was a priestess. And I took excellent care of myself. Abuse was not tolerated by Aziba or by any of us. Self-respect was always our priority.

But prostitution is always painful. It fosters contempt for ourselves, because it assumes that we must sell ourselves in order to survive. It fosters contempt for men, because, as we perfect the art of exploitation and manipulation, we learn to make them want us without allowing ourselves to want them.

I mastered detachment, but more so than in the tents and the tenements, I felt lonely. Among the poor and lowly whores, there was comraderie. We hated our lives, and we admitted it.

With Aziba, we were expected to transcend. Detached from ourselves, we could not share our feelings with others. Thus, detachment from our pain meant detachment from ourselves, and detachment from ourselves meant detachment from each other, meant detachment from God.

I needed love. I needed God's love. But in my desperate need to detach from the anger, contempt and jealousy that surrounded me, in my desperate need to detach from the longings and the disappointments within me, I could never truly feel me, know me, love me, the me in God, the God in me.

I learned this with Reuben, you see, and that was the beginning of my break with Aziba.

Reuben was a beautiful, gentle male soul, with skin like the spirit of a baby lamb and lips like plump dates. And he became my lover.

Aziba did not approve. She encouraged us to empty ourselves of anger and fill ourselves with light, but she feared we would be hurt if we allowed ourselves to bond deeply with men. I think she feared that we would bond deeply with ourselves and find our lives abhorrent.

She was right. As I bonded with and loved Reuben, I could no longer prostitute myself in any way. I became more connected to my own needs, and I needed to be loved without having to seduce or manipulate or sell myself in any way. I needed to be loved by God without having to seduce or manipulate or sell myself in any way.

I began to find in our sacred dances a lack and an emptiness I had never noticed before. I could feel the wind but not the sun, the light of God, but not the heat.

We tried, Aziba and I, to reconcile our growing differences, but to no avail. My spiritual life was taking me in another direction. I needed to feel love for myself and for all being; I allowed myself to feel love for men; I began to allow myself to feel love for God.

More than anything else, Reuben prepared me for Jesus. He was in my life but a short time, yet I was once again deeply changed.

I have lied again, not about the effect that Reuben had on my life, but other things. I will explain all that later. But first let me tell you about Jesus.

Chapter x

I can see from the sparkle in your eye that you are anxious for me to talk about Jesus. My heart beats with a quickened pace, just thinking about him.

God, I loved that man. I was in the process of breaking with Aziba when I met him. Of course, I had heard of him before, but I was too proud to even consider that I might need a man, especially for spiritual guidance.

I had, by the grace of God, accumulated a great deal of wealth despite my youth. I had even helped set up my father in business when he and my sister came to Jerusalem after my mother's death. (My brother had been killed in a freak accident with a horse several years before.)

Are you surprised that I helped my father? I had forgiven him as part of my emptying process, although, as you have seen, I still had some anger clinging to the crevices of my heart. Frankly, too, it was easier for me to set him up in business and be rid of his requests for help than to keep him as a dependent and have to deal with him all the time.

In any case, I had my own wealth, and I owned part of my father's business—that was our arrangement. So I was able to retire at the age of twenty-eight years old, shortly after my relationship with Reuben.

Oh, that's true, I never told you what happened with Reuben. Well, it's quite simple. He left me. He loved me and gave me great tenderness, but he needed a wife and was afraid of my strength and independence. I'm pretending now that it didn't hurt. I'm pretending because I don't want to admit that Aziba was right about that, that to let a man have your love makes you vulnerable.

But it's stupid to pretend. And I was hurt. Yet I can see now, and could see fairly soon even then, that Reuben was a moment for me to open another part of my being and that when he had played his role, both of us needed to go on.

So, anyway, to get back to Jesus. . . .I had heard a great deal about him, but we had never met. But an extraordinary circumstance brought us together.

Remember I told you about our political activities? Well, when I was preparing to leave Aziba's sect and retire, there were many on both sides who began to fear what I would do. You see, as long as I was with Aziba, they trusted that I would abide by the long-established rules of noninvolvement, neutrality and absolute discretion. What would I do if I broke away?

Their fears were ungrounded, totally ungrounded. I had no interest in betraying any of their secrets. I wanted only to be closer to God, my body and my self. Yet fear is such a powerful force, it can overpower good sense and even years of trust.

Friends brought me rumors of my impending doom. Many mornings, I would be in my garden, practicing the lute, meditating, developing new sacred dances that would include the male, as well as the female aspect, and friends would come to warn me that there was plotting against me in the city.

I dismissed the rumors as insignificant. I wanted to deny that anyone but myself would be affected by the proposed changes in my life. I wanted to believe that I could get out of the tangle of prostitution and politics with no cost, without paying for the protection and power I had enjoyed for years.

I wanted to believe that my sisters and clients would be happy for me, that they would not feel as a criticism my rejection of them and the way of life we all shared. I especially wanted to believe that Aziba supported me.

What denial! All parties were now afraid of me. The Romans feared that I would return to the traditional Jewish fold and betray their trust; the Jews feared that I would sell secrets to the Romans; perhaps Aziba feared that my defection implied some fault in her.

There were, of course, meetings. Menachem ben Israel was the Jewish envoy, and Octavius, the soldier with the helmet over his face, negotiated for the Romans. Where did they hold their secret meetings? And how did they know of my plans to retire?

I want to believe that someone other than Aziba alerted the conspirators. I want to believe that Aziba refused to let them use her house, that she declined to give them the details they needed about the way my household ran.

What was the truth? Could she have betrayed me? Did she feel I had betrayed her? Did she refuse to participate directly but allow the meetings because she told herself she was practicing detachment, that she was only allowing destiny to manifest?

What a bunch of camel dung. I suppose detachment can feel like rationalization when the painful destiny is yours. Perhaps any beautiful ideal can be misused by us, human beings, still more motivated by fear and pain than by clarity and love.

You may wonder why those two particular men were chosen or chose to plot my death. Octavius was known to hate me. When I joined Aziba, I refused him entry into our house; he would never abuse me or another woman in my domain. And Menachem ben Israel feared me because of what I knew of his sacrosanct family. His daughter Rachel had fallen into trouble, and he had asked my help to procure her an abortion. Oddly enough, I had come to love Rachel through the experience, and I would never have hurt her. In truth, I had so much shame about molesting his daughter, Basya, I would never have injured any member of his family, not even him.

The conspirators decided to inflame the masses against me with wild stories of my whoredom and child sacrifice. A mob scene was orchestrated. Octavius and the Roman authorities were a major factor in the conspiracy. Without their compliance, the mob scene would not have been successful. But well they knew that their compliance had to appear fortuitous. Had they been a visible part of the events, the Jews and other nationalities would have immediately realized they were being manipulated for political ends.

Aziba, too, had to be totally behind the scenes. She had too poor a reputation to be a convincing prosecutor. And Menachem ben Israel had to appear compelled by circumstances. No one could ever know that the city's aristocracy was behind the plan. Yet his presence was essential to lend legitimacy to the mob.

It was a Tuesday morning in the market, and, as usual, hundreds of people were milling about. Paid instigators started to speak loudly to each other, and quickly they gained a group's attention.

They claimed to have found evidence that I had broken from Aziba and the Jews and had sacrificed a child to some ancient Babylonian God. Menachem ben Israel just happened to be on the scene. As a member of the Sanhedrin, he would have to pay attention to accusations about human sacrifice. As rehearsed, he pleaded for moderation, but was "pressed" by the mob into confronting me.

The mob came to my home and demanded entry. I had always felt safe behind my walls, but this was more of my denial. One of my servants had been paid to let them in. Amazing that I, of all people, should forget the servant's resentment of the master.

How arrogant I had been in the face of my friend's warnings, I, the great priestess, meditating in my garden, feeling protected by great mystical powers. Suddenly dozens of angry men were at my door and I felt afraid. Rough men trampling through my house and snatching me from my room, me being buffeted among them and dragged out of my home, the sanctuary that I had built with so much pain and effort.

I was flung down on the street. I was called whore, adulterer, temptress, witch. . .More stories were recited of my strange cult rituals—my movements, my chants. Allegations were hurled about my bloody practices.

Menachem ben Israel suddenly felt compelled to speak. I, also, had threatened his daughter Rachel, had tried to recruit her into my whoring sect, had frightened her into giving me her confidence, had tried to entice her into ritual sacrifice. The penalty for adultery was death; death by stoning was the ancient law.

I felt stunned. My sin with Basya, so many years ago, began to haunt me. Was it my destiny to pay now for what I had done then? Was the Almighty using her father's treachery to clear my karmic debt?

Confusion and self-doubt began to torment me. I lost my power in that moment, the power to speak, to defend myself, the power to call on God to bond with me in the face of treachery and humiliation. I lost faith in myself, dear friend, and that is the worst betrayal a woman can face.

When I tell you it was a miracle, it was. Out of nowhere emerged a man, not just a man, a man of great strength and love and God, a man who could see to your heart and through your heart, a man who could strip you naked and love what he saw, a man I have loved and cursed, cherished and damned, a man I have betrayed through anger, a man to whom I have been faithful all my life.

The man was Jesus. He instantly saw all the forces that were arrayed against me. And with the uncanny knowing that he had, he looked straight into the heart and eyes of Menachem ben Israel and saw the child molester that ben Israel was. In that instant, he saw a way to save the man's soul, as well as mine. He said to the pious Jew, "Let he who is without sin cast the first stone."

Menachem ben Israel, who had long ago realized that I had been a young child in his employ, one of the many he had molested, Menachem ben Israel stood before Jesus in fear and shame. I had never mentioned our former relationship, and neither had he; but the knowledge of his act played upon his mind, and the shame and the fear drove him to long for my death.

But now, my death would avail him nothing. His guilt and shame were known by Jesus; he could feel it in Jesus' eyes. His guilt was known by a man, a holy man, a teacher, not just by a child, a woman, a whore. Now he would rot in hell if he hurt me again.

"This holy man is right," ben Israel said. "Despite the piety of my home and heart, yet I know he is right. Let us end this madness and go home."

The mob was not so easily dissuaded. They had come for blood, and they wanted blood. But the paid instigators took their cue from ben Israel, and soon they had the good people of Jerusalem on their way home. Except for Jesus. In front of all assembled, he put his arm around my shoulder and walked with me to the entry of my house.

I will tell you much about Jesus and much about our time together. But first, I feel the need to pray.

Blessed be Thou, Our God, King of the Universe, who anointest my head with oil. Blessed be Thou, Our God, King of the Universe, who leadest me beside the still waters. Blessed be Thou, Our God, King of the Universe, who restorest my soul.

Amen.

Chapter xi

A little earlier, I told you that I had lied. The lies were about Reuben. But before I tell you that story and explain why I was so hesitant to tell you the truth, there is a whole chapter of my life that I omitted, and I must come clean.

After Miriam, I went back to the tenements. Between that time and the days with Aziba, I told you that I earned quite a bit of money. Haven't you wondered how? How did I do so much better than the vast majority of prostitutes of the time?

I tried to skip this part, because in remembering it, I once again feel my humiliation. But I find I can't hide anything anymore. While all that I told you about Aziba is true, I felt a certain emptiness in the telling, because I knew I had breezed over a shameful but important time in my life.

Shortly after my return to the tenements, I ran into an old friend, who had left the tents some months before I. Meena Yereva, a strange girl with a strange name. I don't know where she came from. In any case, she looked very prosperous, and I asked her how she had done it. The city was teeming with prostitutes, and the money was not very good.

I had already realized the importance of prostituting yourself to the right people. The act is always the same; but the pay can vary greatly, depending on how desirable you are perceived to be and by whom. If you are a servant's whore, you are nothing; if you are a king's whore, you are desirable.

In order to be a king's whore, however, I needed a queenly setup, a fine place to live and work, beautiful clothes, the right contacts and powerful clients. How could a poor whore, like myself, get established in this way?

Meena taught me, and I was a good student. To get the capital and cultivate contacts, I let it be known that I would give special services to the right people. Quickly, I got into the game, and a shameful game it was. I procured boys for worthy politicians, and while I pretended that male children didn't count, I couldn't quite believe that myself. But worse than that. . . .

Get me a cracker, please. I feel myself weak again, and I need something to eat. Thank you.

I promised myself when I started this story that I wouldn't give a damn what anyone thought of me, but I am becoming attached to you, and this makes me vulnerable. I suppose I need more than food to gather the courage to go on; I need your compassion.

The most significant act of betrayal that I committed in order to elevate myself from the street was a lie I told for a man, a powerful Roman, you would know his name. He was a brutal man, and he had killed a Jewish woman. The death of a woman, especially a Hebrew, was normally not a matter of great concern, but this woman was the daughter of a judge, a power in the city, and an investigation was inevitable.

The Roman's friends approached me. I had already done them a number of favors, and they assumed I would be willing to swear that the murderer had been with me at the time of the killing. I was willing, and I did.

Are you surprised that the authorities believed me, a Jewish whore? They didn't. The whole game was a power struggle between the Jews and the Romans. Everyone knew I had lied, but that didn't matter.

I hate that I did it. Using men and being used by them I could justify in the bitterness of my heart. But I had loved women, and to help cover up the death of a sister made me sick. Furthermore, while I was angry at the Jewish God, I had no love for the Romans, and with this act, I lost any self-respect I had managed to maintain through rape, molest and abuse. Now I was a traitor.

You ask why I did it. Was money worth that much to me? Never. Everything, always, was about God and getting his attention. An ugly and destructive act, a pathetic attempt to spit on God, to show that I could gain power against him by betraying his people, it was a hateful way to catch his notice. Yet in my twisted heart, it made sense. My anger towards God never seemed to affect him, but my betrayal would.

It didn't work. I didn't feel God's anger, much less his respect. With no retribution from either man or God, I felt less acknowledged than ever. I had only my own shame. I can still remember the feel of the silk shawl I bought with the bribe. The soft fabric felt like blood running through my fingers.

It makes me sick.

After that, you know the story. I struggled with that life a bit longer until I could tolerate no more, and then I began my journey to Aziba's door, where I learned to feel God's acknowledgment by surrendering the need for it.

Do you wonder how Jews ever trusted me after I betrayed them, us? I wondered often. I know they trusted Aziba, and perhaps I was cloaked by her reputation. Perhaps me they never trusted, only used. Nevertheless, powerful Jewish men came to me, slept with me, confided in me. Strange. I suppose that betrayal for a price was something they, too, were familiar with. It may even have made them feel more comfortable with me.

In any case, past rumors of my betrayal may have contributed to my vulnerability on that awful Tuesday morning, when the mostly Jewish mob was ready to stone me for adultery and human sacrifice, for the betrayal of Hebrew law. Perhaps every man in that crowd had been a betrayer himself, had betrayed himself, his family or his God for a piece of bread. Perhaps the crowd was stoning the Mary Magdalene who had betrayed them. Perhaps they were stoning that part of themselves.

I would have accepted it as my karma to be killed for a betrayal I did not commit to atone for the many I did. I suspect we all believe in karma because we know, every one of us, that we are never innocent.

But my death was not meant to be.

So let's go on and talk of other things.

Chapter xii

So now, the lie. This brings me to happier days, much happier days.

The lie was about Reuben. His name was not Reuben, it was Peter. And he did not leave me, I left him.

Now, calm yourself. I can see the gleam of curiosity in your eyes. Yes, it was Peter, Jesus' Peter, and I suppose I have felt a bit shy talking about our love for a lot of reasons. First, it was a very intimate experience. Second, few ever knew, and there will be such an uproar when the story is told. And finally, there is a tragic side to this affair, which you will see shortly.

I am so relieved that I told you about my betrayal. I feel a new surge of energy and an excitement to go on with my story.

To protect myself, I have lied in my life. I have even lied to you. But I have rarely lied to myself. And even to you, it has been difficult. I have continually corrected my narrative, because I value honesty, whatever the consequences. Peter, on the other hand, was an incorrigible liar. That was one of his two great flaws. The other flaw was jealousy, and that was a deadly flaw, indeed.

Being a liar, when Peter showed up at my house, he created an elaborate pretext. He was but a naive fisherman in the big city. Some pranksters had approached him in the market and had given him my address. Jesus, they had said, had asked them to find his disciple Peter and to direct him to this address. While he was shocked to discover himself in an infamous brothel, Peter, trusting as he was, would not leave till his master arrived.

What nonsense! The truth was, of course, that Peter wanted to meet me and couldn't justify that to himself.

Peter, Peter. You always wanted to be the perfect disciple. You were so concerned with how you looked, you abandoned how you felt—your feelings, your wants, your desires. Jesus never wanted or needed you to fit some preconceived mold. He needed your honesty. He needed your love. Peter, you could have been yourself. If you had not compared yourself to Jesus and tried to be like him, you could have loved yourself and loved him, as well. Instead you loathed him, as we all loathe those who make us feel ashamed.

The simple fisherman image was one Peter cultivated, but it was another of his lies, a well-cultivated illusion. True, he had been a fisherman at one time, but in the company of Jesus for many years, he had become a fairly sophisticated man of the world.

Jesus, himself, was a worldly man, comfortable with dealing in the political arena. He was never averse, however, to granting his disciples authority, so often, when he wanted to negotiate with the powerful of a community, he would send Peter as his ambassador.

Peter was good at negotiation, and he convinced himself that lying was one of his gifts; that Jesus had chosen him for his ability to manipulate the facts. The opposite was true. While Jesus believed in compromise if compromise were part of the healing process, he despised ruse or subterfuge and continually sent Peter into the fray in order for him to learn that honor and power could have the same home. By the end of his life, Peter had learned this lesson, and I bless him for that.

On that fateful day, sticking to his silly pretext, Peter sat in my anteroom and refused to leave. Liar or not, what a powerful man he was! Upstairs at my desk, I could feel his energy right through the floor.

I suppose I was a bit of a liar then, too, because when I came down the stairs, I pretended that I wanted to get rid of him. In fact, I was excited by his energy and wanted to meet the man who could evoke in me this response.

I feel like a young girl again telling you this bit of my history. Among men, Peter was my first love and my only love, other than Jesus. He was so dear, so gentle, so impish, so full of trouble. He would hold my hand and breathe on my fingers. He would hold me in his arms and make surrender feel like victory.

He was a lusty man. I'm afraid to say that, because it might be misunderstood. He was a devoted follower of the great master, but he wanted desperately to be married, to have children, to create a sanctuary for his roving heart and spirit.

If I had not met Jesus, Peter might have found a different fate; he might have surrendered his role as disciple and followed Jesus as a husband and father. I, too, most likely would have chosen marriage and children, for which I would have surrendered my role as priestess and some of my vanity as well. But I did meet Jesus, and I found myself irresistibly drawn to another path. And Peter felt betrayed by the two people he loved the most.

I have often thought that Peter betrayed Jesus because of jealousy, not because Jesus and I were lovers, but because we were not. Peter suspected, and in a way this was true, that my love for Jesus was stronger because it was untainted by the years of pain I associated with sex, and he felt that our fidelity to each other was more absolute because Jesus and I were bound not only by our love for each other, but by our love for God.

With Jesus, there could be no contest, and that devastated Peter's pride. He could not compete sexually, because Jesus and I did not have sex; he could not compete materially, because Jesus offered me no such support. He could not compete spiritually, because Jesus would not compete.

After I met Jesus, my relationship with Peter changed. It no longer had a future, and we pulled apart. Later, after Jesus' death, Peter and I travelled a hard road together which included the birth and death of our only child. But never, even then, was there a sense that we could be a family.

When I left Miriam and for many years after, I asked myself, am I so obsessed with men that I cannot feel God's eye upon me unless I am surrounded by men? Do I not recognize a woman's love as enough? I was obsessed with men, with their importance in the universe. Yet, had Miriam been a man, I still would have left. Miriam chose to hide, and hiding could never bring me into the center of life, into the center of God.

But self-doubt dies a hard death. Similar questions plagued me when I came to love Peter and knew that I had to leave Aziba's sect. Once again, I asked myself, is it my obsession with men that makes a man's love more potent than a woman's? Am I still a betrayer and a slut, this time selling out for men's kisses rather than for their coins. There was no truth to this. Or was there? I know I left Aziba not because she was a woman, but because she was afraid to love. Had she not been afraid, the test woud have been a true one, but now I suppose I'll never know.

And then, as I let go of Peter as my lover, I asked myself, was I so obsessed with God that I could not feel acknowledged if I were with a mere mortal? Did I need God's very son? Was I so dazzled by the vision of a master that I could not love an ordinary man? Or did I abandon Peter because I was afraid to be loved completely, as a woman? Did I use Jesus in order to avoid marriage? Was I afraid to give up the image and autonomy of the priestess, a role I had worked so hard to achieve?

Did I sabotage my chance for a longlasting sexual relationship, because sex still brought up in me shame too powerful to release? Did I need to hold myself aloof from ordinary women? ordinary men? because I still felt like a whore, like a molester, like the dust that God neither hears nor sees?

Did I abandon my life, my direction, my happiness, to find an illusory place in the center of God's heart? Was I, thus, still a prostitute, now God's personal slut?

I will not go on tormenting myself with these questions. I will tell you today, tonight, that I left Peter simply because I loved Jesus more. And since, by his choice, Jesus and I could never be man and wife, I chose to be his mate on whatever level I could, chose to share his fate, to hold his heart in mine, to kindle his spirit and be sustained by his faith.

Peter, long in your grave, forgive me for betraying our love for another. Your heart and hand healed me, brought me out of an emotional desert. Your love stirred me out of the cold, ascetic spirituality of my mystic detachment. It bathed me in the love of man and the love of God.

Yet, on that Tuesday morning, my illusion of invulnerability shattered by an angry mob, I met a man whose eye could penetrate my soul and whose silence could wash away the years of self-abuse. On that Tuesday, I met a man who needed most what I most wanted to give, myself in my simplest and truest form.

57

Peter, you were a marvelous man, but you were not my peer. You lied to yourself, as I could not. You protected yourself, as I did not. I was a whore, a molester and a betrayer. Yet as a whore, a molester and a betrayer, I struggled to find my God.

In Jesus, I found my peer, a man willing to go through the depths of pain to find his soul, a man questioning and requestioning himself, a man more afraid of the lie than the truth, a man who could love, a man whose life was consecrated to his relationship to God.

Peter, you followed Jesus because in him you saw a great light. I walked next to Jesus because with him I more clearly saw my own.

God, as I approach my death, I forgive Miriam and I ask her forgiveness. I forgive Aziba and I ask her forgiveness. I forgive Peter and I ask his forgiveness.

So be it. Amen.

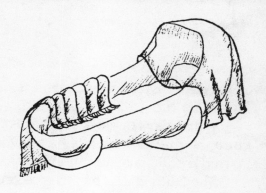

Chapter xiii

Umray nadj, Umray nadj, Umray safir, maleki hadj. You don't recognize this song, do you? It's a lullaby from my childhood, something my mother used to sing.

I suppose that I have villified that poor woman. I haven't told you anything good about her. Well, there were good things, and it's strange that at this moment as I approach my death, I feel myself wanting to rock once more in my mother's arms. I want that peace again.

Peace was something that I do not associate with my years with Jesus. While he was, at times, deeply peaceful himself, his life was not, and I shared as many moments of his life as I could.

You have that look in your eye again, the look that means, Mary, tell me everything. Well, my friend, I would like to tell you everything, if only because I would like those wonderful moments to be my dying thoughts, but to tell you everything would take years of remembering, and we haven't that much time, at least I don't.

I will tell you things that strike me now, the funny moments, the tense ones, the moments of doubt, those of joy. I remember, for example, how I used to complain about his habits. My God! Was he disorderly. You wouldn't think it, would you? But he simply paid no attention to the details of his life, and I was enraged because he was so like other men who expected women to look after them.

I both resented and loved taking care of him. I designated for him a room in my house, and he came there often after long days of work or weeks of travel. I always greeted him, no matter how late he arrived, and I personally prepared a bath to restore him body and soul.

The truth is that he never asked me to care for him. He would have loved me whatever I did or did not do. But so many people used him, lived off his energy, I think I felt moved by his own unmet needs and wanted to give what I had. Perhaps it made me feel important to be needed by such a man. Perhaps to some small degree I was still a prostitute, not trusting he could love me for myself alone.

Complaining about him did make me feel important, because complaining implied that we had a relationship. I especially liked to complain to his mother, and she, in turn, liked to tell me about her tribulations.

Mary was an incredible woman—tough is the word that most readily describes her. She had had ten children, including Jesus, and always she had struggled with the family's endless demands. Her husband needed and merited her attention; Jesus had always required special treatment; and nine other siblings had to be cared for and made to feel as important as their extraordinary brother.

On the rare occasions that Mary was in town, we would exchange stories about her marvelous son. Sharing our experiences made Mary and me feel close, and talking about Jesus helped soothe me when he was away.

Joseph, too, was a wonderful person; he would be seen as a saint in your age. What made him so extraordinary is that he had both humility and a powerful sense of himself. Unlike so many of us, Joseph had transcended the need to compete. He humbled himself before his son, adored his wife and kept himself out of the public eye. Yet at the same time, there was nothing obsequious about him. On the contrary, he trusted himself and valued his place in his own and God's eyes.

Of course, they had their flaws. Mary was perhaps a bit too pushy, and Joseph perhaps too permissive. Yet, all in all, they were an inspiration: a loving couple, a man and a woman who had achieved some equality between them, parents who could love themselves in the face of such a son. I can see why God gave them to Jesus and Jesus to them.

Jesus rarely criticized anyone, but he loved to tease his mother about her constant worry, a habit she claims to have acquired when she took the family into Egypt to protect Jesus from Herod's death edict. It was a harrowing tale, how Mary carried Jesus into the desert and Joseph stayed home until Mary with their new son felt safe enough to venture home.

There were other sons, and I am afraid that jealousy abounded. Despite Mary and Joseph's efforts, the other sons felt slighted and belittled. This pained Jesus terribly, and he rarely talked about it. Sometimes I wondered if his need to surround himself with male disciples wasn't in some way an effort to compensate for the rift that existed among them. In any case, he ran into jealousy with the disciples, as well; now instead of brothers competing for their parents love, these were brother disciples competing for the love of God. Like Peter, the disciples failed in their own eyes; and also like Peter, they were angry at themselves and God, their self-loathing creating a womb for betrayal in them all.

I think Jesus felt this to be his failure. While he preached self-love, even he could not find the key to ignite it in other people's hearts.

Jesus had a great sense of humor and a great sense of delight. He loved to see people's joy when he helped them. I'm sure you have heard of many of his feats: raising people near death, healing ills, providing poor folk with relief from their sorrows. Once he stunned a whole congregation by turning water into wine.

People loved him more often for what he did than for what he was and taught. He knew that. Sometimes he would question these "miracles" and their value.

"I want to teach faith," he would tell me at night after his day's labor. "Yet I think sometimes I am having the opposite effect. People base their faith on what I do, rather than on God's love. Perhaps it would be better to do nothing."

Yet he almost always gave in to the impulse to help people. If he saw a need and felt he had the means, he would work the miracle, even while calling on people to trust themselves and God.

Jesus worked tremendously hard; he always questioned himself, searched for the truth, sought God's direction in everything he did. Examining himself and extending himself to others, that was his life.

Physically, he was quite small, but tremendously strong. He needed that strength, walking as he did from sea to mountain, from desert to village, walking and talking, giving what he had and gathering strength as he gave.

I often accompanied him on his journeys, though it was exhausting. He did not care much about physical comfort, and he could walk further than was humanly possible. Even when travelling with a troop of us, he spent a great deal of time by himself, so I was often lonely as well.

Travelling with him was always worthwhile. I loved to hear him speak and preach. And I was always moved by the looks of astonishment and gratitude that were sure signs that he had touched a place.

Do not misunderstand. Jesus never used his power just to please a crowd, and he was far too honest to be popular for long. Sooner or later, eager followers would become disappointed, and disappointed followers become enemies.

I remember, for example, a wealthy and powerful gentile who approached us one day on the road from Galilee. To my amazement, the nobleman had begged Jesus to let him become a follower.

"I, too, am a man of God," he had said, "and I weary of my worldly life. Let me join you, and I will help you achieve your work."

Jesus did not hesitate. With one hand, he touched the man's shoulder, and with the other, he touched his third eye. For Jesus, it took less than these simple movements to know a man's soul.

"Go home," Jesus said. "You fool yourself. You have left your family to feed your pride. You would better serve God by humbly feeding your children. Confront yourself and your responsibilities. See why you are afraid. Work this out with your wife, and then come to me."

The man cursed and went his way, and Jesus had a new enemy, and a powerful one at that.

Jesus made many enemies. He would not pander to please, and he rejected all offers of political power. This enraged many, for men who do not want power are hated by men who do.

But it was not his enemies that betrayed Jesus; it was his ambition. He craved a power that belongs to no one, not even to God; it is the power to save people's souls.

Jesus lacked detachment. He wasn't willing to allow people to suffer the consequences of their actions. Many betrayed him, and he knew they would; yet always he tried to protect them. Many used him, and he knew they did; yet always he allowed them.

You wanted to be the savior, Jesus, and you didn't care what it cost or who.

I hate you for the crucifixion, the great drama where you waited expectantly for men to set aside their fears for you. It was arrogance that caused you to be shocked when the masses abandoned you and your friends deserted you. It was arrogance to think they would put you before themselves, that they were ready to transcend their fear because of your need. It was arrogance to think they should.

And it was arrogance for you to ask God to forgive your tormentors. What right did you have to ask God to forgive another? How dared you ask God to change another's fate for your sake? Still playing the savior, you tried to intervene in destiny once more.

Everyone has been blamed for the crucifixion except you. But it was your show. You created the script. You timed your acts. You picked your role.

And who did it cost? Us, your mother and I, faithful to the end, there for you, when you were not there for yourself. We had to witness the betrayal; we had to witness the pain; and we had to know in our hearts that you were wrong.

It cost your followers. They were like children, following your lead. Your arrest was an abandonment for them, and in your absence, they showed their weakness. Too undeveloped to act out of self-love, they acted out of fear. And when they saw their terror and betrayal in the face of your crucifixion and pain, they fell into great confusion, great self-hatred and great shame.

And it cost the earth, because collectively mankind has borne the blame.

You went on to glory, and we have had to deal with the aftermath—the sacrifices made in your name after your death, the imitators wanting to be saviors themselves, the leeches hoping you will usher them into the kingdom of heaven, and, worst of all, the multitudes who have bought the lie, who are still waiting for you to save them.

Did you ever notice the irony? Only two of us stood by you at the cross, but innumerable martyrs followed your death. Hordes of people, throwing themselves to the lions, dying for their image of themselves, dying because they believed they could get into heaven on your coattails, and yet not one to stand by you in life, because no one could abide you alive.

You were abandoned in life and worshipped in death, because no one could abide you in life, because no one could feel his equality with you and God in the face of your compassion, in the face of your love, in the face of your connection with God.

Do you know, my friend, why we alone, Mary and I, stood by him till the end? It's because only we acknowledged that he was a man. Only we saw his faults, so only we could be with him and maintain our self-love and self-respect. Because we did not abandon ourselves, we did not need to abandon him. Because we honored our own relationship with God, we could honor Jesus, love Jesus, have compassion for Jesus, stand by Jesus, even when he was wrong, even when he was hurting us. And he hurt us.

Jesus, we didn't and we don't need a messiah. You cannot be our savior, because we need to save ourselves. You have no right to try to take responsibility for our fate, to live for us or die for us. To do so is to degrade, humiliate and disempower us.

We could have walked a different path together. Jesus, you could have let go of being the messiah. You could have accepted your humanity and ours. You could have helped us deal with your life, rather than your death. You could have let God and mankind interact as they were meant. You could have rendered unto God what was God's, rendered unto mankind what was mankind's, rendered unto Jesus what was Jesus'.

Jesus, forgive me for saying these things to the world. Too long have I kept these thoughts to myself and protected your memory. Death is coming to our era, the era of Jesus Christ, as we knew him. And it is time, past time to make an accounting of ourselves and to release the earth from its guilt.

Do you understand what I'm saying, Beth? I'm saying that for nearly 2,000 years the earth has carried the anger and shame of the crucifixion. And it's time to let them go, to be free.

It's time for each one of us to become our own savior and neither try to save another nor pull on others to save us. It's time to see Jesus' choice as his own and for us to let go of our shame. It's time to let Jesus off the cross and to let the earth off the cross as well.

And now I see it is time, past time, for me to stop raging at God, because it's time for me to stop raging at Jesus. It's time for me to stop blaming him for escaping from the conflicts of his life, for trying to be more divine than he was. And it's time for me to stop blaming God or you or myself for his death.

When Jesus died, I died. I felt lost in my grief, lost in my heart, lost in my soul. I had lost my connection with God, not because I had lost Jesus and he was my connection, but because my anger with him, with God, with everyone and everything, grew like a cancer and killed the love that I had begun to feel for myself, for God, for all being. And once I had lost God, and once I had lost love, there was nothing more to lose.

I brag about my detachment. I claim to have had more than he. And yet I see how long I have grieved and raged over his death, over his betrayal of me, of who I wanted him to be.

In truth it is I who made Jesus the messiah, because I could never forgive him his wanting to be. No less than the others, I have created a savior, only to crucify him. I have set up a leader to love and then to abandon. I have let him be a symbol of perfection, and then perfection betrayed, rather than a man simply to love, regardless of his faults. I have taken responsibility for him, for what I deemed were his mistakes, so that I could avoid taking responsibility for my own.

It's time for me to allow Jesus to die, wounded in his soul. It's time for me to respect his need to learn in his own way. It's time for me to acknowledge that his life and death were perfect, part of my own evolution, his, the earth's.

And I say to us all, it's time for us to surrender our guilt. It's time for us to bless God for allowing us our mistakes and Jesus, his. It's time for us to bless ourselves for making them. It's time to honor our path, forgive ourselves our pace, allow each other to fall, offer each other our faith. It's time to bless ourselves for being human.

Jesus, join us again. Walk with us, in front of us, behind us and beside us. Point the way for us, and let us point the way for you, as we struggle to be, to surrender, to allow and to love. Come down off the cross, and follow your heart to God in the company of those who love you and love themselves.

Jesus. Forgive me my anger. Forgive me my pain. Thank you for your willingness to love. Thank you for your willingness to bleed. Thank you for your willingness to learn with us and for us. Thank you for your willingness to be part of our great endeavor, the healing of the earth, the healing of God, the healing of ourselves.

Amen.

Chapter xiv

There used to be a tiny shop where artisans made the most exquisite sandals. Two days after I met Jesus, a worker from that shop came to my home and fashioned me a pair. It was a gift from Jesus.

Jesus knew the sandals would mean a great deal to me. On the day we had met, he had accompanied me back into my home, and there we had talked for hours, sharing intimacies, offering each other our histories.

On that day, he had washed my feet. I had always hated my feet; their smell and shape had always embarrassed me. Jesus must have felt that shame. How like him it was to sense my vulnerability and to honor that part of me that I most despised.

I loved the sandals and wanted to offer something in return. But how could I return the gift? Jesus needed nothing but my love and my ability to share his vision. A book, an article of clothing, nothing I could think of would mean as much to him as his gift had meant to me.

Finally, I realized how to delight him. I would arrange a feast for his disciples, who happened to be camped nearby. The best food and wine, some charming entertainment, the festivities would be a break for the men, whose lives were hard and lacking in the smallest luxury.

The evening was a great success, and the men clamored to meet me. Even before the feast, the disciples were curious about me. For months, they had been hearing about Mary Magdalene through Peter, and recently Jesus had recounted to them the tale of my rescue from the mob.

The thought of a connection between themselves and the infamous Mary Magdalene also titillated them. While they did not live in Jerusalem, they were in and out of the city often enough to have heard my name, and to the men of the times my name meant wealth, power and the promise of the night.

The night of the feast, Jesus promised his disciples that he would soon invite me to the camp. And so the following sabbath, I came to sup.

I shall never forget that evening. There was a warm breeze, and from a distance, I could smell the bread baking, sweet and tempting. We had a simple meal of bread and goat's cheese, but sitting about in that circle, I felt an incredible contentment. Here was a group of men who were neither leering at me nor planning how to use me, a group of men who loved their leader as I was beginning to.

While Jesus' followers came and went, there were a few who stayed year after year, and I met a number of them that night. Immediately I think of Mark, a resentful youth with a huge scar dividing his cheek. He loved his master; he was always transformed in his presence.

And then there was Matthew, a man born to be either a chronicler or an accountant. Among the whole group, only he was organized and fastidious, and he managed to keep Jesus' life and living conditions in some kind of order. Since I liked to play the caretaker role as well, there was a bit of rivalry between us. But it was mostly Matthew who took care of Jesus and the whole crew, and I had to admit a tremendous respect for him. Orderly in mind, as well as body, Matthew kept meticulous notes on Jesus' life, but unfortunately many of his writings have been lost.

Another that I remember well is Judas. A man of power and means, he was nonetheless a fierce defender of Jesus and a promoter of him as well. He loved Jesus like a brother but could never feel at ease with himself in the younger man's presence.

Unfortunately, the wonderful comraderie did not last. As Jesus and I became closer, the disciples came to resent me more and more. When in Jerusalem, Jesus often stayed with me, rather than with them. When I travelled with him, he turned to me for support more so than to them.

The jealousy that was natural under these circumstances was exacerbated by my being a woman. First, there was probably sexual jealousy. Not all of the disciples were celibate; as you know, Peter was not. And I was seen to be one of the most desirable women of the time.

There was also anger that Jesus would relate closely to any woman. The disciples, on the whole, wanted to keep women in their place, and it galled them to see me treated with reverence and respect. Rumors abounded that I was using my femininity. Unwilling to acknowledge that Jesus and I could love each other as equals, some of them gossiped maliciously, saying he was using me for sex and that I had seduced him.

To Jesus, celibacy was not a principle, but in his own life he felt it to be a requirement. He could never be promiscuous, and he feared that an intense sexual relationship would bond him too much to the earth and distract him from his destiny. I was disappointed by his decision. I wanted to be totally bonded to him and have him bonded to me. But I accepted his need for freedom and enjoyed the tender closeness we were able to achieve.

The inability to integrate women was a grave weakness of the disciples. Although women occasionally travelled with Jesus, he did not allow us to join on a permanent basis. He feared the men would become distracted, that they would fight with each other for dominance and that there would be constant discord, with the women struggling for equality and the men resisting it.

I think, in the end, the sexual segregation was a mistake. Trying to resolve the inevitable conflicts might have matured the disciples, and perhaps the presence of women would have resulted in greater stability.

In any case, I wish I had been allowed to join. Perhaps, then, the other disciples would have resented me less. Our living situations would not have been so dramatically different, with me living in luxury, them in tents; and they would not have felt deserted by their leader every time Jesus wanted to spend time in my company.

Sometimes I think Jesus wanted to keep me at a distance from his daily work. He may have needed a place to go to get some perspective. He may have needed my home for his detachment and peace of mind.

Despite our living apart, and despite his endless travels, our friendship developed rapidly. From the first, we both felt deep trust in each other. And also from the first, neither of us doubted that our connection was destined to be.

The timing was right for me. The experience with Peter had opened me to a new level of vulnerability with a man and with God, and with Jesus I could take those final steps. Without hesitation, I concluded the process of breaking with Aziba, and I was quickly able to let my girls go to her house and to retire from prostitution forever. I still had a few minor business ventures, but they required little of my effort, and keeping them enabled me to support myself comfortably.

I was able to devote nearly all my time to propagating Jesus' vision of God. For that was our mission: to teach that

God loves us, no matter who or what we are, and that knowing that God loves us is all we need to know.

Jesus used to say, "Love is the healing power. To the degree that you love yourself, God and others, to that degree you will be healed." A gentle prophet, Jesus eschewed the fire and brimstone teachings of the day.

I loved his message. And because it resonated in my heart, I knew it to be true. With great energy, I strove to bring this message to women and to Jewish women in particular. I chose Jewish women, because among them I found easier acceptance. While I had had a great deal of contact with men of all nations, I had had less contact with their wives and daughters. And those few I knew were likely to despise me because of my profession.

Of course, Jewish women often hated me, as well. But the bonds among our people are strong. They are like family bonds, hard to break no matter what the offense.

I also worked a great deal among prostitutes of every nationality and description. Despite my desertion of the profession, I was well loved among these humble of the earth. They admired both my success in the business and my ability to give it up.

Jesus, too, found himself teaching mostly to Jews, but that was not by his own choice or design. With a few important exceptions, non-Jews were not drawn to us, and Jesus never forced himself on those who were not ready to hear.

At first Jesus had no problem with the establishment, either Jewish or gentile. While confrontive to each of us individually, he did not care to attack the whole political and social structure of the time.

Despite these intentions, trouble was inevitable. Many of his followers and would-be followers wanted him to become more involved in the political arena and were offended by his refusal. Judas was among them.

While not political enough for some, he was too political for others. It was simply his way to give respect to all, regardless of their nationality, sex or station in life.

Unwilling to be used in the political game, Jesus' very being was a political statement; it was an affront to those who cherished rigidity and order in society. Those who supported the occupation were against him, and so were those who opposed it and who wished to impose a new order of their own. Those who taught us not to question the law were against him, and so were those whose rebellion was a grasping for power.

Jesus threatened the way we deluded ourselves. Our image of ourselves crumbled in the face of his rigorous honesty, his unselfconscious treatment of all life as equal in value to God, his ability to see and communicate with the God within all being—men and women, children, animals, insects, trees, stone, the sea.

In the presence of Jesus, each one of us saw ourselves more clearly. That was why he had to die.

Jesus' allegiance was always to God and to himself. He sought no allies, only friends. And he feared no man.

He didn't care whom he offended. He didn't care that his relationship with me outraged his disciples, the Romans, the Jewish establishment.

He always treated me with respect and love, and I came to feel an equal in the eyes of God and mankind. I, Mary Magdalene, a prostitute, a madam, a trader in state secrets, a woman, a molester, a liar, a betrayer, I was equal to God, because I was of the essence of God.

Through Jesus, my dream was realized, and I will worship and adore and exhalt and revere him until I die and beyond my death. Because now, instead of being dust in the house of my father, I was an honored and respected sister in the house of God.

Blessed be Thou, oh God, King of the Universe, who has raised me from the dust, who has pierced my eye with the eye of the falcon, who has pierced my spirit with the spirit of the angels, who has pierced my soul with the soul of Jesus, of God, of the eternal light.

Amen.

Chapter xv

$\mathfrak{I}$ don't know how I'm going to be able to finish this. When I try to speak of the crucifixion, the grief wells up in my throat and I cannot speak.

Give me a sip of water, will you, Beth?

My energy is slipping away, again. It is almost as though I would prefer to die than to go on with my tale. But go on, I must, if only to release the pain once and for all.

For painful it was.

I am glad we talked earlier about Jesus' ambition, that I was able finally to forgive him and love him once again. But that anger has been a great defense for me, my friend, and now with it gone there is no buffer between me and my pain.

And painful it was.

You know the story, at least most of it. His enemies were too many; his friends too weak; his will too conflicted. His desire to be the savior was the energy that won, that moved him toward his death. It was his last effort to turn around humankind, to force a rebirth of the human spirit. It was his final act of will against the will of God, who was detached.

They took him, the Romans. I was frantic. His mother came immediately from Nazareth, where she and Joseph had continued to live. Peter was nowhere to be seen; nor were any of the others, except one of Judas' servants, who loved Jesus and brought me news.

I used every contact I had made. I went to Menachem ben Israel and reminded him how Jesus had saved his very soul. I went to Judas and begged him to redeem himself by using his considerable funds. I went to Pontius Pilate, himself, and threatened to reveal secrets that he hoped would die with him.

To no avail. Pontius Pilate claimed to be unable to stop the course of history, but the truth is he wanted Jesus to die. Judas claimed he had not betrayed Jesus' whereabouts intentionally, that he was sick with grief, but he wanted Jesus to die. Menachem ben Israel said he had no power with the Sanhedrin, with the Romans, with the mob, with the army, but he wanted Jesus to die.

They all wanted Jesus to die, because who could abide the day of his coming? Who could stand when he appeared? Who could tolerate the falcon's eye? Because he was like a refiner's fire, not in that he burned us to hell with self-righteousness, but because he melted our hearts with love and self-honesty.

Quickly the hours, the moments moved. I panicked. Gone was the detachment I had spent years to forge. Desperately I searched for a way to stop the unstoppable.

Into the night, I cried out to God. If you love me, God, if you love him, stop him, stop them, stop yourself.

There was no relief. Helplessly I stood by and watched him stoned, abused, condemned, despised by those to whom he had offered only the love of God. Helplessly I waited for him to act, to use the power I knew he had, to fly over the gates of hell, to join me in the middle of the night so we could run away to anywhere, to the mountains, to the sea, to oblivion, I didn't care which.

He would not run. I knew that. In my mind's eye, I remembered him in all the ways I had come to know him: tired and discouraged, empassioned and optimistic, clear, confused, enraged, compassionate. Never running.

When he was but a child, he had studied with all the great rabbis of the time. Each one had welcomed him, not because of his scholarship, though that was prodigious, but because of the love of his courage and the courage of his love.

This was not a man who could escape or run, not when he believed that his sacrifice would be the turning point of civilization.

The walk to Calvary was an agony. Soldiers, hecklers, a sneering crowd accompanied him to his death. Followers and sympathizers there were, too, meekly observing the crucifixion of their savior. How could these humble folk stand up to Caesar when Jesus would not? Stunned by confusion, feeling abandoned, they could not understand their leader's passivity.

Why had he abandoned them? Why did he not break his bonds and reveal that God was the greater authority and that he had the power of God? Why was he not changing destiny itself?

Confused, hurt, the wretched of the earth clung to the same hope that I did, that he would stop the charade, that he would strike his tormentors with a great bolt of lightning, that he would fly off the cross, legs straightened from their grotesque pose, flesh meshed in health and well-being, matted hair now spun with a golden light.

It didn't happen. Do you understand? It didn't happen. And all who were there and all who were not there trembled with a fear more enormous than the fear of death itself. Because the powerful, who had feared his mighty hand, had more to fear when he did not use it, because now it was not Jesus, but God himself they would have to face. And the meek—his disciples, his many followers —now isolated, alone, without his guidance, they, too, trembled with fear, because now they were without him, because now without him, they had to face themselves and God.

Hours of agony, and only two of us, his mother and I, surrounded by guards who joked casually, because they, too, felt ashamed and afraid and did not want to be there. Hours of agony, with our heads bowed so that we did not see the moment of his death; we only felt a wrenching and then a peace, a release, a surrender by the man who died on the cross, a cross of his making, who suffered in righteousness and self-doubt, even at the end.

And we knew his suffering, because we spoke, the three of us, on and off, when the others had gone. And he told us of his pain and his agony and his disappointment. And we assured him that his sacrifice would not be in vain. And we assured him that our love for him was a symbol of the love that millions would feel for him forever. And we assured him that God saw him and loved him for his anger and his pain and his struggle to forgive.

It was the only time I ever lied to him. Because I did not believe. I believed only that I loved him and that my death would have been an easier thing to bear. I believed only that I loved him and that my love was not enough to comfort him in his sorrow and his pain. I believed only that I loved him and that God was the heartless bastard I had always thought him to be and that to be human and vulnerable and frail made us the cosmic joke devised for the entertainment of a gallery of gods who did not see and did not hear and did not care. I believed only that he had failed me.

Jesus, forgive me, because I abandoned you, no less than the others. My heart, full of anger and pain, did not, could not accompany you to your death. It failed to bring to your dying moments the love and laughter you had brought to my life.

I have never confessed to another human being this sorrow and this shame. But on this day, before you and before God, I beg you, Jesus, to forgive me for abandoning you, for letting you go because I wanted you too much, for cutting myself off from God, from the only source whose love could have sustained me, whose light would have been enough to share with you.

Jesus, forgive me. And in this moment, let me make amends. Let me rain upon you the love that I have from and for God and the earth and myself. Let me share with you my faith in you and God and the earth. Let me bring to you the blessings of our people, that has roamed the earth for thousands of years, looking for the key to our deliverance, a key that we can only find in our hearts and in our relationship with God.

Jesus, let us be once more together. Let me not turn away. Let me look up at you and see you at the very moment of your death. Let us pray.

The Lord is my shepherd, I shall not want.

He maketh me to lie down in green pastures, he leadeth me beside the still waters, he restoreth my soul.

He guideth me in the paths of righteousness for his name's sake.

Yeah, though I walk through the valley of the shadow of death, I will fear no evil, for Thou art with me; thy rod and thy staff, they comfort me.

Thou preparest a table before me in the presence of mine enemies.

Thou anointest my head with oil; my cup runneth over.

Surely goodness and mercy will follow me all the days of life, and I will dwell in the house of the Lord forever.

Amen.

Chapter xvi

It's a wonderful feeling to be reunited with Jesus again. Thank you for the period of silence. He and I needed to be alone.

I can see the moon rising for me. I am almost at life's end, and I want to die.

It's hard to stay here now, to talk about the past. With peace in my heart, there's little attaching me to the earth. Yet I feel the need to share a few more things before I go. More amends, perhaps, especially to God.

Mary and I stood together by the cross, yet we did not share what was in our hearts. Perhaps had I had the courage to tell her of my rage, I would have found a way to release it. But as it was, I stood next to her, yet apart from her, from humanity, from God.

She did not speak either. I don't wish to cast any blame. She may not have needed to speak; she may have felt at peace. I needed to talk, to share, to expose the viperous feelings that I chose to hide.

Two guards had kept vigil with us. And though they were soldiers of Rome, they were not unkind. One in particular, I still remember his eyes, full of pity for Jesus, for his mother and for me.

Mary and I asked the kind soldier to take Jesus' limp body down from the cross, and the man, himself, offered to help us carry Jesus' body to its resting place.

Mary and I realized that we had not acknowledged that Jesus would die. Where would we bury him? I knew of a cave not far from where we stood, and we agreed to have the soldiers help us carry Jesus to his crude burial ground.

The body was repulsive to me. Suddenly it seemed frail, whereas in life, it had always seemed so robust. Devoid of his spirit, it mocked us with its vulnerability, the savior now reduced to flesh already in the process of decay.

I do not remember much of that procession: two Roman guards, Mary and me. Along the road, we met Peter. Dear, frightened man, he was already seeking ways to make amends for his acts of cowardice. Peter and I dismissed the soldiers, and now the three of us continued on our way.

Once we had reached the cave, we met Joseph. He had followed Mary to Jerusalem, and while he arrived too late to see his son's agony, he had discovered our destination from the soldiers who had helped us. Rushing ahead and by a different route, he arrived more quickly than we, burdened as we were with his son's body.

I remember so clearly the tenderness Joseph showed to us all. Mary was sick with grief, and her husband begged her to go home and leave the burial itself to Peter and me. I concurred.

Frankly, I was ashamed of my thoughts, of my anger toward Jesus and my anger toward God, and I would have been happy to have been alone. But Peter's help was needed, so I pretended to be pleased to share these terrible rites with him.

From the moment of Jesus' death until this one, I ceased to speak the truth. For there is no truth when one's heart refuses to reveal itself. And one lie leads to another, as I came to see.

With great reluctance, Mary let Joseph lead her away. She would be back. But for the moment, she needed rest and the comfort of one who had been with her through the whole history. Once again, I envied them.

Mary, I hope we will be together now, now that I am free of anger and deceit, now that I am willing to reveal my heart. I want to know how you felt on that terrible day. I want to confess that I threw myself into abysmal isolation. Did your children, your husband, your own inner strength keep you from surrendering your life to dread and emptiness? Or did you, like me, hide your feelings and suffocate in your own lies?

Peter and I brought Jesus' body into the cave. It was dark and dank. Silence abounded. Peter, wracked with shame, sat in worshipful silence. I, wracked with anger, sat in rageful shame.

At one point, there came a miracle. Jesus seemed to rise out of his body, and he looked straight at the two of us.

Frozen with terror, fearing his accusations, Peter and I clutched hands and awaited eternal judgment. But none was forthcoming.

"Thank you for this thankless vigil, my beloved Peter and Mary," he had said. "I need a great service from you, and I ask your help."

Who was this? It was not Jesus, not the man I had loved so deeply in my heart. This was a miraculous vision, but one empty of feeling, of power, of being. I would have been relieved had he castigated me for my desertion; I would have been willing to beg for forgiveness had I felt his anger.

But this being was too far from me. He was my savior, but he seemed to have forgotten that he had been my lover.

"In this work, you will be blessed," the image of Jesus continued. "Go to my disciples, and gather them together. In three days I will come to them and you; in three days, I will be resurrected. Because I am not dead, not in spirit, and once I have risen, all doubts will be dispelled."

Did he really say these things? Did he use these words? Try as I have, I cannot distinctly remember. So anguished was I, so alienated from him through my anger, my pain and my shame, I barely grasped his words.

Peter leapt into action. Finally, he saw a way to redeem himself, maybe even to punish himself for his betrayal. I lifelessly followed him, compelled by duty? by the need to cover the truth of my feelings?

Whatever exactly he said to us that night, the essence was that we were to gather the disciples at a certain place and to await his appearance among us. The teaching of the true and loving God must go on. He was not dead in spirit, only in body.

Who cared? Peter's enthusiasm sickened me. I knew it rose more from guilt than from self-love. In that, Peter never changed; always he aimed to be that perfect disciple.

There wasn't very much for me to do. Alienated from the disciples because of our history, I did not wish to be close to them now, did not trust them with the exposure of my heart. And they, thinking they had been shamed by my fidelity and devotion, shunned me more than ever before.

We gathered, the disciples and I, at the appointed time, and Jesus did what he had promised. He stood among us and spoke of our work. He appointed Peter the head of a great endeavor, to spread the word. He spoke to us in tones of compassion and love. True to his beliefs, he forgave even Judas and asked God to forgive.

The rest is history. The news was spread. Even I did my part, telling the tale to the women with whom I had worked.

But nothing mattered to me anymore, and I wanted to die.

Probably I should have gone to Aziba and asked for her help. She was the master of detachment, at least when it came to the lives of others. But I resented her too much. Maybe I was too proud. In any case, I didn't do it.

Empty, empty, empty. I began to sicken in heart and soul.

Peter and I revived our old relationship, but it contained nothing of its former energy. United by shame, we were both dead, though he would never admit the truth of how he felt.

The next years were full of preaching and politics, but I was little involved. With Jesus safely dead, hundreds of people joined our little sect, and soon the authorities were after us.

I was pregnant again for the last time. Friends advised us to go north, to Europe, to preach, to teach and to escape the persecution. I feared the journey would jeopardize the baby's life, but I hated too much to care.

We travelled on foot, by sea and on foot again. In a cold cave, somewhere in southern Europe, we set up a camp. There were five of us: Peter, Luke, Saul, Jacob and me. And soon there was the baby.

It sickens me to tell you this. I had my baby. Finally, I had my baby, a little girl. In a cold Spanish cave, I had my baby, and I let her die. I couldn't feed her. My soul had dried up, and so had my breasts. My baby, my little girl, dead, and it was I who had killed her. It was my anger, my shame, my self-hatred, it was the poison of my silence that dried my breasts and starved my child.

I have asked her forgiveness many times. And I have asked the forgiveness of God. I ask forgiveness again.

Soon I will see her. I long to smile into her little face and smell her baby breath. I long to fulfill myself as a mother, as a giver of life.

I don't know what my future holds, but if I return to earth, I hope to have a different sort of path, a more ordinary

84

life with ordinary bonds. I want to attach myself to things, to people; I want to know that kind of love.

But now I must complete the life I have been destined to live and honor the choices I have allowed myself to make.

I became very sick, Beth. My skin turned into sores, my bowels into bloat. I begged Peter to take me home. I wanted to die in my own land. I wanted to taste dates in my mouth; I wanted to smell the sea.

It was time. Peter, too, wanted to go home.

We travelled, I with death beckoning, Peter with despair at his heels. We travelled, and as we travelled, Peter began to change.

I believe he forgave himself. I believe he let himself atone for his sins —for his jealousy, for his fear. I saw in his eyes a light, and I felt his self-love ignite in his heart.

I wanted to praise him. I wanted to tell him I understood. But so many years of silence between us stood like a great mountain between my heart and his. I never did speak of it.

Peter, I want to tell you now how much I admire you, how much I respect your willingness to walk the tortuous path of your life. I want you to know how you began to inspire me again with the words you spoke along the way to our ancient homeland, how I listened along with the many or the few and how I felt the stirrings of God one more time within me.

How petty it was of me to deny you that praise. How ugly of me to always hold myself above you. In those last moments of our life, it was you who had transcended me; it was you who had found the great light.

To all the disciples I make amends. I mocked you all, disdained you all. When Jesus was alive, I thought you weak; when he was dead I thought you full of self-deceit.

Who have I been to judge? Judge not so that ye may not be judged.

Lord, I have sinned. I have sinned the sins of pride, of vanity, of judgment.

As I face my death, God, I ask you to forgive me for the sins that I committed knowingly. I ask you to forgive me for the sins that I committed unknowingly. I ask you to forgive me for the sins I committed from weakness. I ask you to forgive me for the sins I committed from negligence.

I ask you to forgive me for the sins I committed from fear. I ask you to forgive me for the sins I committed from shame. I ask you to forgive me for the sins I committed from loneliness. I ask you to forgive me for the sins I committed from the pain of my anger and the anger of my pain.

I am leaving the earth, but now I know that I will return. I feel within the earth the stirrings of a new vision, and I want to be part of that destiny.

God— more maligned than I, more abandoned, more desecrated and more in need —I commit myself to the healing of my heart, I commit myself to the healing of my soul, I commit myself to the healing of you and of our earth.

Be with me, as I commit to be with you. Stand by me, as I commit to stand with you. Walk with me, as I commit to walk with you.

God, I forgive and I ask your forgiveness.

Amen.

Epilogue

Mary Magdalene died suddenly. I felt her narrative to be incomplete, but she and God had found their reconciliation, and in their wisdom, they released her from the earth. Through our time together, I had grown to love her. Now it is I who must accept the loss.

About the Author

Life prepared her to write *The Autobiography of Mary Magdalene*, believes the author, Beth Ingber-Irvin. A woman of wide-ranging experience, from social activism to mysticism, Beth has known the journey from abuse to struggle to surrender to forgiveness.

A gifted channel, Beth has worked since the early 1980's as an intuitive counselor and teacher. Always developing more powerful tools for healing, in 1986 she co-founded The Healing Partnership, a California center for the practice and teaching of intuitive counseling.

Beth's special relationship with Mary Magdalene started when she was fifteen and culminated in her writing Mary's autobiography. Currently she lives in the country, where she continues to expand and deepen her work, while at the same time healing her own relationships with husband, partners, animals and God.